MONSTER MAN

By the same author

LA Postcards
Stoked!
Radical Take-offs

GLYN PARRY

MONSTER MAN

A Mark Macleod Book
RANDOM HOUSE
A U S T R A L I A

For Sandra

This work was assisted by a writer's fellowship from the Eleanor Dark Foundation. The author gratefully acknowledges his time in residence at Varuna.

A Mark Macleod Book
Random House Australia
an imprint of
Random House Australia Pty Ltd
20 Alfred Street, Milsons Point NSW 2061

Sydney New York Toronto
London Auckland Johannesburg
and agencies throughout the world

First published in 1994

Copyright © Glyn Parry 1994

All rights reserved. No part of this publication
may be reproduced, stored in a retrieval system,
or transmitted in any form or by any means,
electronic, mechanical, photocopying, recording
or otherwise, without the prior written permission
of the Publisher.

National Library of Australia
Cataloguing-in-Publication Data
Parry, Glyn, 1959- .
  Monster man.

ISBN 0 09 182900 3.

I. Title.

A823.3

Cover design by Donna Rawlins.
Typeset by Midland Typesetters, Victoria.
Printed by Griffin Paperbacks, Adelaide.
Production by Vantage Graphics, Sydney.

Out there in the darkness,
out there in the night,
out there in the starlight,
one soul burns brighter than a thousand suns.

street fighting years
Simple Minds

PART ONE

'It's just all of a sudden, boom, like lightning striking.'

A parent

'It is definitely a crime of thought—he is very organised and has rehearsed the modus operandi in his mind many times, and although his victims are random the situation is very structured.'

Paul Wilson, criminologist, commenting on the abduction of two Sydney teenagers

THURSDAY LUNCHTIME

Samuel Levine wandered into the kitchen for more coffee. Plenty needed to be done before Saturday morning: the house key, the purse, all sorts of supplies. Darwin was some journey. They would be on the road for the best part of a fortnight. Through the kitchen window he eyed the driftnet of cumulus. He filled the kettle and switched it on. He'd just remembered: breakfast cereal. What brand did sixteen year olds like?

Soon the kettle hissed steam. He heaped a spoonful of Nescafé into a mug, poured in the boiling water and walked back to the study. He scanned the vacant lot. It was a wild looking place. Earlier he had seen some kids sneaking around down there in the long grass. He thought of snakes.

Across Daybreak Drive and onto the school oval, two hapless boys collected up cricket gear while the rest of the class stormed the gym. He dismissed them all. Boys were the same wherever you stopped.

Ah, but Melanie Spence was a different matter.

He threw open the top drawer of the desk and grabbed a pen and his writing pad. He kept the writing pad for Claudia. He wrote every month—long, perfect letters—but she never replied. Maybe she wanted to go on punishing him forever. No matter. All would be forgiven on Saturday. He could imagine her astonished looks.

See, Claudia. I kept in shape. I didn't go soft in the belly like some brothers do.

He wrote the word FUEL. Monster scoured the house looking for him. Levine detected its stinking presence as it seeped from room to room. How much fuel? He settled on a full tank and a jerry can. That would get them safely to Geraldton, just under 600 kilometres north. Then he would do it all over, again and again until they reached the Northern Territory.

Was that the school siren? Levine dropped the pen and pushed the writing pad aside. The itinerary could wait.

He sensed Monster close-by now, moulding itself to the contours of the passageway, all hunger and thirst, and he knew the time had come. Soon Melanie would appear on the school oval for lunch. Beautiful Melanie.

Rachel hadn't realised the Surfmasters was that week. As they drifted onto the grass the talk centred on Margaret River.

'Hey, Melanie, what are you wearing for the social?'

Angela often took the topic away. It was a get-Rachel tactic that usually worked.

But not today. Rachel launched into her big sister routine. 'Just ignore her. Must be a desperate phase they go through.'

Angela shot back. 'Not as desperate as hanging around slopes.'

'Hey, I already warned you. Leave off, okay.'

'Sure.' Angela opened her lunchbox and took out an apple. 'Only last term you said we should keep Australia for Australians.'

'They *are* Australians! Live in the real world for once.'

They found their usual spot near Daybreak Drive and sat down. Across the vacant lot some year tens waded deep into the summer grass to share something heavier than a packet of Marlboro.

'Yesterday some creep was watching me outside the public library.' Melanie spoke softly; she knew how it would sound.

'Lucky you,' said Angela. 'Did you get his phone number?'

'Hey, I'm not joking. It was scary.'

'You mean the guy was some kind of pervert?' asked Rachel.

'I'm not sure. I think so.'

'So tell Brad. He'll sort him out.'

'Yeah, sure. And then what?'

Rachel shook her head. 'I don't believe I'm hearing this. What did he look like?'

'Dunno. Intense, I guess. Weird.' Melanie studied the ground. An ant dragged the brittle husk of some other insect. 'I went inside the library. I made like I was doing an assignment or something.'

'Yeah, well I'm off to the canteen.' Angela stood up and brushed dry grass from her skirt. 'All this sex talk is making me hungry.'

As she walked off Rachel fired her a dirty look that would have flattened Manhatten. It had no effect.

'Do you think I should tell someone?'

'Nah. Why bother? You'd only look dumb.'

Melanie conceded. She was about to switch the conversation back to tonight's social when a red Ford Falcon S-Pack pulled up onto the verge, its engine loud and meticulously tuned.

'The master calls. Catch ya later, Mel.'

'Look, I'm real sorry.' Melanie eyed the car and wished she could make life simple again. 'You know Brad doesn't like it when I keep him waiting.'

'No worries. Sit next to me in biology. We'll talk then, okay.'

'Sure. Hey, I'm fine. Really.'

'Sit next to me anyway. I want every detail.'

'About the creep?'

'About the weekend, silly! Tell Brad he has to drive back for you Saturday morning or else. It's only fair.'

'Yeah. Whatever.'

'And Mel . . .'

'I know. No more fights, right?'

'Something like that.'

Monster wanted to get going to the shopping centre, to flick through the magazine racks at the newsagency. Lately it liked the skin art magazines with their tattoo exhibits of flesh and neon ink. Levine ignored Monster. He was too interested in watching Melanie. Sweet child of the universe. Had she ever been north before? Could she even guess at the sheer size of the big sky country?

See the sky, Claudia. See how big it is.

He suspected Melanie had never really looked at the night sky. No matter. Soon all that would change. At midnight on Saturday she would kneel down beside him in the silent wheat crop, feel the warm earth between her toes and know there were better worlds to be had away from the highway. She would meet Claudia.

He watched her with the boyfriend. The boy looked a sleaze, like he only wanted Melanie for one thing. He didn't like to think of her even talking to scum like that. All boys were the same nowadays. She deserved someone better. Claudia had deserved someone better, too, but she hadn't listened. She'd run off with the wrong types.

Melanie hoped the siren would go. She hated these drawn-out silences of his.

'Brad, please. You know I can't say yes.'

He combed his fingers through the tangle of his

hair and said nothing. He didn't look at her. It reminded her of the way her father had behaved last year before he'd walked out for good.

'I'm going. If you're just going to stand there.'

She watched him dislodge a clump of grass with his heel. Didn't he care about getting grass stains on his new Rivers?

'Look, I'll see you when you get back.'

'So what is it?' Brad finally acknowledged her. 'Upper school? Your stupid mother?'

'What you're asking is impossible. Be fair.'

He leaned back on the Ford. Melanie moved closer. She reached out and took his hand. At least this time he didn't resist.

'Try and understand. Please. For me.'

'So what's to understand? You do whatever your mother tells you to do. End of story.'

'No I don't.'

'So say you'll be ready if I come round for you after school.'

'Brad!'

'Okay. Forget it. Forget us.'

'Brad, please!'

'Nah, it's time we killed it anyway.'

'All because of Margaret River?'

'Not just Margaret River. Your mum. School.

Everything. It's no use.'

'No, wait.'

The siren. Great. She fought the impulse to hurry off to the lockers. Biology, followed by private study in the library. So boring. But she couldn't wag.

Now Brad watched her coldly, seemed to read her mind. 'See! Hey, if you'd rather run back to class, that's fine with me. Be a little schoolgirl.'

She let got of his hand and stepped back. 'There you go again. Always twisting my words.'

'Yeah, babe. Whatever.'

'I've had this.' Melanie started to go. She didn't have to stay. If Brad couldn't cope with the situation, that was his problem, not hers. But the Surfmasters was definitely off.

'Probably scared I'll try and get into your pants again!'

'What did you say?' She spun around, angry, not caring anymore.

'You heard.'

'You're a turd, Brad.'

'Yeah, yeah.'

'A real loser. You're just like my dad. All you care about is yourself. You couldn't care less about anyone else.'

'Bye, Melanie. It was nice not knowing you.'

She couldn't stop herself. She marched up to him and punched him hard in the chest.

'Hey!'

'Get lost!' She punched him again and hurt her hand. 'I'm through with little boys messing up my life!'

He grabbed her wrist and pulled her hand away. She struggled, kicked, saw that he was grinning down at her.

'It's not funny, retard!'

'Melanie!' He grabbed her around the waist and pulled her in close. 'Quit hitting me, okay.'

She didn't want to quit hitting him. She wanted to hurt him, really hurt him, make him yell. She saw how dumb she was being. Suddenly she couldn't move. She stopped trying, allowed all the anger to go out of her and Brad relaxed his grip.

'That's better.'

'Sometimes you make me so mad.' She felt ashamed. 'Did I hurt you?'

'Nah, I'll live.'

'I hurt myself.' She flexed her fingers. 'Ouch.'

'Here, babe.' He pulled her close and she knew he would win, that he always did.

'Please try and understand. I really have to get

back to class. Drop by later if you want. Mum's working late.'

He ignored her. She allowed him to kiss her. Maybe everything would still be all right. His hand moved up onto her breast and he turned her around, away from the school.

'Brad, not now. Not here.'

'Shush, babe. Don't wreck it.'

'Brad, please. The siren's gone.'

He turned the purse over. Here was the prize. Silly Melanie. She really should listen to her teachers. But yesterday afternoon outside Ashmere Public Library she had left the purse inside her school bag and the rest had been easy. He'd guessed there would be a house key.

Samuel Levine drank the coffee slowly.

Melanie was the only reason he had stayed on in Ashmere. He'd found her by accident across town in Big W. That was Monday afternoon, just as the store was closing. He had rushed in to pick up a five-litre pack of Castrol GTX2 and had made his way to one of the checkouts. She was in front of him being served. He made a note of her school uniform immediately. She turned to say something to the checkout operator and he snapshot the image.

Perfect! She and Claudia might have been twins.

Back at the car, Monster roared at him to forget her and drive up the coast as planned. Western Australia was some mean road map and they were nowhere near finished. He tried to describe her and Monster screeched. The abuse got so bad he thought his head would burst and he had to switch off the motor. Then he saw her again, crossing the car park and heading for the bus stop. He begged Monster to quit the noise and just look at her, dammit.

Monster looked.

Monster liked what it saw.

He could have driven over to the bus stop, snatched her off the pavement and driven away, but rejected the idea. Sheer impulse. Safer to have a plan. That was why on Monday afternoon he worked out his response carefully. He watched her climb onto the bus for Ashmere and discreetly followed her home.

Later he found Collie River, parked on the reserve and slept under the stars. He dreamed of a girl with golden wheat in her hair, of wind chimes and whale song, of immortality. Beautiful Claudia.

TAKING CARE
OF BUSINESS

Every afternoon the crows flew in for a free feed. Empty chip packets and half-eaten sandwiches littered the school.

'You know what gets me the most?' Melanie didn't wait for a response. 'The way he always just stands there and makes like it's my fault.'

Rachel sliced another section of leaf and scraped it onto the viewing slide.

'I mean, what am I supposed to do? Just drop everything and jump in his stupid car?'

Outside two crows fought over the remains of a pizza slice.

'I don't even *like* surfing. And I definitely don't like some of the cases he hangs around with.'

Kids started to pack up their experiments.

'Hey, you're not listening.'

'Here.' Rachel made room for her. 'Your turn to look. But you'd better be quick.'

Melanie stepped up to the microscope. All she saw was green nothing.

'One minute, class. Let's go. Everyone back to your seats.'

'Already?' Melanie glanced at the clock high above the teacher's bench. 'No way. Did you see the way he drove off?'

Rachel gave a sly look. 'You weren't complaining when he kissed you.'

'You saw that!'

'Me and half the school.'

'Hell. Was that all?'

'You mean did I miss that mighty right hook of yours?'

'Oh, no!'

'Don't worry about it. Did he say anything about staying on for the social tonight?'

'Nah, him and the mob want to get away by seven.'

'Then you'll need a lift home.'

'What happened to your dad?'

'Busy. Some kind of dinner talk in Bunbury. Me

and Angela are grabbing a ride with Sue. She could drop you off afterwards.'

Melanie thought about it.

'Safer than walking.'

'Nah, forget it.' She tapped her ruler on the bench. 'Just don't tell my mum or she'll spin out.'

Rachel wiped the viewing slide clean and put it back in its box. 'Here.' She handed over what was left of the leaf. 'Bin this.'

'I know what you're thinking, but you're wrong.' Melanie dropped the leaf onto the floor and kicked it under the bench. 'Just because we made up I'm not going to change my mind, okay. No way am I going to Margaret River. Maybe next year.'

'Yeah, maybe. If Brad's prepared to wait that long.'

Melanie watched an empty corn-chip packet roll across the lawn. 'He keeps nagging to see that hot video I told you about.'

'The porno your old man forgot?' Rachel packed away the microscope. 'Lucky you. Pray your mum never finds it.'

They walked back to their bench and opened their work files. Outside the crows were leaving already.

Levine walked across the car park to Ashmere Village. The sky was ruffled linen. It made for a pleasant afternoon: humid, but not too hot. He reminded himself to order some flowers, just like Clint Eastwood.

Outside the Commonwealth Bank he inserted a credit card into the automatic teller. He checked the PIN number scrawled down on a scrap of paper squeezed inside his wallet. The four numbers reminded him of the need to take care. Life was a clenched fist that wanted to smash you down. He sighed and punched the right buttons. Underneath the PIN number he had catalogued the falling account balance. Tomorrow he would run the balance down to zero and throw the card away.

He removed the cash, credit card and advice slip from the machine and walked into the shopping centre, 400 dollars richer and with a wallet already bursting at the sides. The shopping centre was uncrowded. At the newsagency he bought a teenage magazine. Monster stayed with the tattoo magazines while he searched for a decent book, something uplifting to last the journey. He found only rows of gaudy paperbacks. What sick minds designed covers like that? Someone ought to build a bonfire and clean up the mess.

At Mitre 10 he bought an assortment of goods: four metres of thick cord, a jerry can and numerous other items. Satisfied, he walked over to the Mr Minit booth.

'What can I do for you, mate?'

'Last night our young fella pushed the back door key down the septic.' Levine fished around in his pocket and handed over Melanie's key. 'Wife's been nagging me to grab another spare.'

'No problem.' The guy behind the counter thumbed the switch on his bench-top grinder. He worked fast.

Levine noted the time. 15.05. School finished in ten minutes. He wondered if Melanie had missed her purse yet. Maybe not. At lunchtime she'd had the boyfriend to sort out. The purse was disappointing. All it contained was her student concession card, a five dollar note and the usual jumble of schoolgirl trash.

The key was ready in no time. This was the real reason for taking the purse, of course. To get the key cut. Taking the money was the smokescreen he needed to avoid her suspicion.

'There you go. Just keep this one out of reach.'

'Reach?'

'Septics can be costly.'

'Oh, yes. The young fella.' Too late. The guy behind the counter glanced his way. Was he suddenly alerted? Maybe he would turn the moment over to the cops, say, *Well, as a matter of fact I did notice this one customer*.

But no, he suspected nothing. Levine handed over the money, took the key and walked over to the manager's office. The woman behind the desk hardly noticed him. She took the purse and said she would ring the school right away. She promised. He knew she would.

The last few minutes of private study usually meant silent reading. Melanie didn't mind so much. Mr Reynolds allowed magazines.

'So what's happening?' Rachel leaned across the table.

Melanie pretended to be reading a fashion article.

'Mars calling Melanie. Come in, Melanie. Over.'

No good. Rachel caught her smile and she surrendered.

'That's more like it. So did you change your mind yet?'

'Get real. The school would have a meltdown.'

'But you've wagged before.'

'Yeah, and look where it got me. Anyway, I'd miss the social.'

'Wow. Real groovy.'

'Rachel!'

'You should lighten up, Mel. Really. You're sixteen now. Year elevens get to do things.'

Sometimes it felt like sixty.

Rachel got off her case. 'Hey, I'm just wearing my Levis. For tonight.'

'You'll get arrested.'

'Very funny.' They swapped magazines. 'By the way, you forgot to tell me if the pervert actually did anything.'

'Him! Nah. Just stood there watching.'

'Pity. I've always wondered what it would be like. You know, going with an older man and everything.'

'Right.'

'So tell me. Has Brad made it to second base yet?'

'Hey, I already told you. That's for me to know and you to find out.'

Mr Reynolds walked over.

'Reading's boring, sir.' But Rachel was ignored anyway.

'Urgent message for Ms Spence at the front

office. Go to it, champ.'

Great. Melanie closed the magazine and got up. She wanted to ask what it was about but Mr Reynolds was already two tables away sorting out the boys.

'Betcha it's the cops. Brad's taken Admin. at gunpoint and he's refusing to talk to anyone but you.'

Melanie scraped her chair across the floor. 'Look, I'll catch you tonight.' She headed for the door.

'Hey, Mel. Can I borrow the porno? It might give Renny ideas.'

Someone laughed. The library aide took notice. She did not smile.

Coco Pops. Melanie seemed like a Coco Pops kind of girl. Levine remembered they had been Claudia's favourite when *she* was sixteen. He dropped a 750-gram box into the trolly and moved onto the jams. Strawberry? Cherry?

The little girl stopped him dead and he hoped Monster stayed in the newsagency. She was a small piece of heaven. He grabbed the strawberry jam and pushed the trolly down the aisle towards her. Her mother hadn't even noticed him. She was too busy scanning for specials.

Samuel Levine knew this little girl. He understood the childish dreams that cartwheeled through her head. A good little girl. Nice, but only to look at. Mustn't touch. Remember what Mumma said? But years ago Mumma died. A faulty gas stove exploded, knocking her unconscious; before anyone could get to her, fire consumed the tiny kitchen and burned her clean away. Bye, bye, baby. He didn't cry. Big boys don't cry. That's what the cowboy would have said.

He reached alongside and smiled. The little girl smiled back. He pushed his trolley into the next aisle and promptly forgot her.

Ashmere Village loomed ahead. There was no way her purse could have just fallen out. Unless it hadn't fallen out at all. Great. There went the money for tonight's social.

Late-night shopping. No wonder her mother hated being rostered on. Across town the Forum would be even busier. So many Big W specials to kill for. She stepped into the manager's office.

The receptionist stopped typing. 'Can I help you?'

'I'm here to collect my purse. Melanie Spence.'

'Oh, that's right.' The receptionist swung around in

her chair and opened the drawer beside her. She hesitated. 'Sorry, but I'll have to get you to describe it for me.'

'Sure. Small, brown leather with a silver clasp. And there's a chain with a silver M attached.'

That satisfied the woman. She produced the purse and handed it across the desk.

Melanie checked inside. The money was gone, just as she'd figured. But at least the back door key and her student concession card were still there. Lucky break.

'Is anything missing?'

'I don't think so.' She wasn't in the mood for sympathy.

'Well that's good.'

'I guess so.' Now it was Melanie's turn to hesitate.

The receptionist noticed. 'Was there something else?'

'I was just wondering where it was found.'

'He didn't say.'

'He?'

The woman eyed her suspiciously. 'Are you sure there wasn't something else?'

Melanie faked a smile. 'I kinda hoped I might be able to thank him, you know. For being so honest and everything.'

'Oh, sure. But you're out of luck. To tell the truth I didn't pay him much attention.'

But it's your job to pay attention, lady.

She turned to leave.

'Oh, there was one thing.'

'Yes?'

'His boots. He wore these fancy boots, you know. Real cowboy material.'

'Thanks.' Melanie left. The chatter of typing resumed behind her.

Outside she cut through the busy car park. She lingered outside Plains Video. Jumped when a car horn blasted from just a metre away.

'Sorry.'

The vehicle came in slow, slow, almost crawling alongside and she relaxed, half expecting to see Brad sitting behind the steering wheel. He didn't trust her to hang around the shopping centre. Too many others guys, he said. Only—right make, wrong model. And this one was white. She blushed, stepped back onto the kerb as the panel van squeezed through.

The driver turned away, but Melanie knew he'd been staring. Creep. So many men did that, looked then pretended they hadn't been looking at all. She gave him the finger.

PROMISES

He should never have listened to Monster. That way Claudia would never have left. For days his asthma had been playing up and when she'd said she was going away somewhere—anywhere—to get away from Ellendale, Monster had called him weak, spineless, no good. He'd begged Claudia to stay where she was, not to move, not to take one step towards that door. She had left anyway. Left him and Mumma. Six weeks later she'd phoned. She'd said it wasn't all Ellendale and she needed to see him. Alone.

But why dwell on the past?

Driving over the crest of the hill he saw what Melanie must have been seeing all of her life. Suburban Ashmere, with its roofs and trees and buckets of landfill. How many secret places were stored there: creeks, cubbyhouses, playgrounds and that wild assortment of childhood memories? When Claudia was young, before Ellendale and Mumma messed her head up, she had loved him. But then she'd said she wanted to run away. They had turned his own sister against him. Bad. Very bad. What was a good cowboy to do?

Melanie started the long walk home. Boring. If only she had her driver's licence already. Cars made everything look so easy.

'Hey, Mel!' Angela cycled into view without slowing down. 'Brad's looking for ya! He's really pissed off you weren't waiting at home.'

'Hell, didn't you even tell him I had to go to the shops?'

But Angela was already leaning her mountain bike into the fast bend and racing down the hill.

Melanie swore. Just then a red Ford sedan passed her at speed, climbing the hill and surging into top gear as it disappeared over the crest. Wrong again, unless Brad had just had a sex change.

She had to stop beating herself up like that. The last thing she needed was to start thinking like her mother. Who needed to be *that* lonely and scared? Dad. So gutless. One day she would phone him up, reverse charges, and tell him exactly what she thought.

Surfboards packed tight on top of a Kombi. Melanie recognised the mob long before she saw their faces. The tinny horn sounded sick, like it belonged on top of a junk pile, but it did the job and she waved without thinking. Up front, sandwiched between the driver and a guy from TAFE, sat that new girl everyone was talking about, the party animal who got rushed to hospital to have her stomach pumped. Stupid fool. In the back seats Melanie counted three more couples. One of the year twelves bungled a browneye as the Kombi sped past.

Forget it. Brad could keep the Surfmasters. The last thing she wanted was to be stuck in a field, a pub, a car park in Margaret River for three days listening to them all dribble on. Let them all get busted again. Brad, too, if she was being honest. It wasn't like he owned her.

Or was she just being a fool herself?

She started walking again, angry, depressed. What she needed was some of Brad's rap music. He said she should get into it. She pulled her

Walkman out of her bag and snapped to PLAY.

No one noticed the stranger pull up on the verge of Ashmere Park and get out to walk. There was nothing unusual about that. People walked there every day.

Every street in the immediate vicinity was connected to the park by a series of pedestrian laneways. Levine enjoyed the exercise. Two streets later he was there.

He carried a canvas bag, walked briskly up the steep driveway and through the side gate. On Monday afternoon, after following Melanie from the bus stop to her home, he waited long enough to see which entrance she used.

No dog barked. No neighbour observed the hand turning the key in the back door.

Good.

He entered the house and closed the door behind him. The laundry was tidy. An archway led directly into the kitchen. Small. Functional. He counted only two cups on the sink. What else? The heavy drapes in the front rooms shut out the late afternoon sun.

Three bedrooms, with the end one converted for sewing. Melanie's room looked out onto a shady patio area and some lawn. The room itself was small but comfortable, that kernel of privacy every teenager sought.

Levine put the canvas bag down and nudged it under the bed out of sight. The Minnie Mouse doona amused him greatly, as did the Betty Boop figurine on the dressing table. Did girls really go in for all that stuff? Then he remembered Claudia's infatuation for the Road Runner. *Beep-Beep*! He noticed the photograph. Melanie and the boyfriend both fooled around for the camera, their arms wrapped tightly around each other as they leaned back on the red Ford. He flipped the photograph over and laid it face down.

Melanie's wardrobe revealed only two full-length dresses and each was hardly worn. He guessed she didn't go to many parties. She didn't seem like the type and he was glad. If you were careless you got a reputation and boys wrote your name down on their scorecard.

But not Melanie's. He would not allow her to suffer the same fate as Claudia. The boys in Ellendale had written down her name. Animals. Dirty, no good hounds.

Still, one dress couldn't hurt. For Sundays, the Lord's day. Levine remembered it was a hot

Sunday when he had tracked his baby sister down. After the intensity of those last six weeks, Mumma's fury and all, he'd been glad to get out of the house, the whole stinking town. Driving out to meet her had been like leaving behind a bad dream: primary school, railway crossing, general store, pub, solitary Ampol pump. Ellendale. Amen for the oceans of gold further down the line.

No one saw him park the car. Claudia had worn pink and they'd drifted along the dusty limestone track. She'd talked. He'd listened. The sky had looked so big and the air had felt so warm and Monster had lumbered behind them.

She started up the driveway. Just after Christmas her mother had talked her into using the back door. That way the neighbours wouldn't see them so much and that meant they wouldn't gossip so much. Sucked. Dad was the one with the problems, a real deviant. So how come she and Mum were the ones left behind to live with the shame? They should have climbed up onto the roof together and shouted it out for the whole of Ashmere to hear. Instead there was only silence. Dumb, but Melanie went along with it to keep her mother halfway sane. So why couldn't she just accept the fact that

Dad wasn't coming back? Men were bastards. Why blame yourself for their stunted growth?

She looked up at the house next door. The old man wasn't watering his garden or pruning his precious shrubs or throwing down another bag full of woodchips. Small miracle. Mum actually *liked* him! Brad wanted to carve a 360° right through his precious native plants and permanently stop him whingeing about the noise the car made. One day she might not be able to stop him.

She opened the side gate through to the back garden and took out her key. At least whoever flogged her money hadn't ditched her purse into the bush. One thing bugged her. Why stop at five dollars when she had her Walkman inside her schoolbag? *And* the rap tapes she'd bought to please Brad. Real dumb. Not that she was complaining.

The key turned easily in the back door lock. Melanie dropped it back in her purse, picked up her schoolbag and hurried inside. All she wanted was to get out of her school uniform, have a shower, change, grab something from the fridge and be normal.

At last! Levine listened. Melanie's presence filled

the house and he felt intoxicated. He heard the Walkman. Didn't she know she could damage her hearing with that thing?

Later. Right now he squeezed into the tall slice of shadow behind the bedroom door and waited. How long? Ten seconds? Twenty?

Suddenly, beautifully, she was there. She walked right past with her back to him, but it couldn't matter now. The Walkman gave him the edge.

Such beautiful hair, exactly like Claudia's at that age. Would these be the first of many delicious similarities? He hoped so.

Melanie half-turned to face the dressing-table mirror. He was ready to leap out of the shadow but there was no need. She hadn't seen him. God, but she was even more beautiful close-up. He wished he could take her by the hand, sit her down beside him and tell her how much he cared for her. Would she respond to his touch?

Beautiful Claudia.

He mouthed his sister's name in shadow. Unseen, he watched as she toyed with the necklace she wore to school. More than once this week he had noticed the silver M glinting in the lunchtime sun.

She sat down on the bed and started undoing

the buttons on her school blouse. Paused. Stood up. He couldn't see what it was without pushing the door ajar and revealing himself. Something. He sensed Monster growing tense, taut, straining to fill in the shadow, wanting to fill up the whole room.

Now she reached down for something on her dressing-table. Levine thought desperately hard, tried to reconstruct the way the dressing-table looked before his fingers roamed over her things. His fingers. Photograph! She was examining her precious photograph, picking it up now, turning its glossy surface right-side up.

The phone rang. He flinched as Monster mushroomed in size, rushing up the wall and across the ceiling, a grotesque mouth rapidly assuming shape and substance directly above Melanie's head.

No!

Melanie turned, listening hard. She pulled her earphone to one side, put down the photograph and stepped past him into the dining room. The cotton blouse fluttered, revealing her perfect shape.

Monster spared him. He heard its hissing throat recede into shadow, watched its dull vapour slowly peeling back across the ceiling and into the space behind the door.

'Mum, I'll be fine. Really.'

Melanie glanced up at the clock above the kitchen sink. She wished she could get off the phone and get on with her life.

'Yes, but what about getting home?' Her mother sounded tired. 'You know I don't want you walking alone that late.'

'It won't be late.'

'That's what you said last time.'

'Last time was different.'

'No it wasn't. And anyway, it's just not right for young girls to be out walking the streets after dark.'

But it's all right for boys? Sure, Mum, whatever you reckon.

'It's not safe,' her mother continued. 'Anything could happen.'

'Yeah, I forgot. The lions have escaped. The sky is falling.'

'Melanie!'

'You should listen to yourself, Mum. It's so embarrassing.'

So often their conversations came to this. Was it widespread or had she been singled out for a special dose?

'Look, I'll grab a lift with Rachel and Angela. They can drop me off at the end of the street on their way through. It's no trouble.'

The voice on the line faltered. 'So I can expect you home no later than 11.15?'

Melanie remembered the last social. Her mother got bent out of shape just because she walked in seven minutes late. Seven minutes! But how was she to know Rachel had volunteered her and Angela to stay back and help sweep the gym?

'Sure, Mum. 11.15.'

Some kind of store promotion played in the background. Pay day. Big W sounded crowded already.

'Look, Mum, I'm running late. I had to go down the shopping centre to pick up my purse. I'll explain later.'

'Melanie?'

There was a pause while her mother debated the rights and wrongs.

'Mum, I'm going. I'll catch you later.'

She ended the call and wandered through to the bathroom. As she reached back to unclip her necklace she hesitated.

Something, but she couldn't be sure. She listened hard. Nothing. Just her mother's paranoia rubbing off.

She took off her necklace and placed it on her towel. It would feel great to get out of her school uniform at last. She turned on the hot water tap and was about to turn on the cold when something turned her around.

Hey, quit it. This wasn't funny.

Just the roof timbers cooling and creaking. Houses threw strange parties once the sun started going down.

She turned on the cold tap, not too much, and adjusted the temperature. Even in summer she liked her showers steamy hot. Satisfied, she bent down to untie her shoelace. As she did she heard Brad's car turning into the driveway. Typical. Would he be in another foul mood? She quickly switched off both taps, grabbed her necklace and hurried out of the swirling fog into the passageway. She was buttoning up her blouse when she realised.

Too late.

The hand was there so fast that she didn't have time to scream.

THURSDAY NIGHT

No one at Big W enjoyed late-night shopping. Pay day meant there was always a long line of customers wanting to make a payment or pick up their goods or put another special on lay-by. Mrs Spence was glad to be working out back.

'Oh for the Lotto life.' She stepped over a twelve-speed mountain bike one of the casuals had left half-assembled on the floor. 'My feet are killing.'

'Here.' Her offsider passed an unboxed large Esky. 'See if you can find a home for this. Still need a lift?'

'Please. Now they reckon it's going to cost over 600 dollars.' She made a space for the Esky. 'Yesterday it was just a blocked carbie.'

'You should get the famous Brad to look at it.'

'Him!' Mrs Spence laughed. 'He'd probably take the thing apart and sell it for spares.'

'He was in here earlier. Him and his no-good surfie mates. In sports goods.'

'Probably trying to steal a trampoline.'

'It isn't funny. I heard something about him the other day.'

Mrs Spence ticked off a list of items in her file. 'I'm listening.'

'Just that he's been in trouble again. For possession.'

'Save it for on the way home.' She wasn't in the mood, Melanie or no Melanie. Brad worried her. Why couldn't he be someone nice?

Samuel Levine studied the sky above Ashmere. Someone had wiped the night down with an oily rag. No matter. They would be leaving soon. The cowboy left. He died.

He headed through the pedestrian laneway and back to the park. Up ahead he saw the panel van bathed in the soft glow of streetlight. Ashmere Park was empty, children and parents long gone. Even the joggers had finished their run for the evening and finally surrendered to their fast-food diet of tv and ignorance.

He snapped his fingers and breathed in deeply. He reached the panel van and checked the street once more. No one. Not a living soul. Even Monster seemed less volatile after the brisk walk. He was glad. When the boyfriend showed up the situation could have turned nasty. No matter. Soon he was steering into Melanie's street. Outside her house he slowed down, braked, shifted into reverse and carefully backed up the steep driveway into the carport. He switched off the headlights and killed the motor.

When he walked through the house for the second time that day he knew the layout intimately. He worked quickly and quietly. First he carried out two heavy-duty bin liners containing the bulk of Melanie's clothes. He decided against going through the laundry basket. Pushing open the back flyscreen he walked to the carport, unlocked the rear of the panel van and threw the bags up front.

Melanie's turn. He went back inside. Carefully, he leaned over her and lifted her up. She gave out a little groan as he cradled her in both arms but he knew she would not wake just yet. The mixture had been strong. He carried her out to the panel van and gently placed her on a thin mattress of foam, quickly closed both doors and hurried back inside.

One minute.

Final check. First Melanie's room, where he decided against taking the schoolbag. Her school days were over. He straightened up the Minnie Mouse doona, snatched up her precious photograph and closed her door behind him. Bathroom? No need. The rest of the house looked fine. Satisfied, he closed the back door and checked it was locked. He shut the side gate, got in the panel van and fired up the motor. Slowly, and without headlights, he drove to the end of the street.

Two minutes, maybe three at the most.

He flicked on his headlights, turned left and joined the mid-evening traffic. He would drive into Bunbury and celebrate with some take-away. Everything had gone so smoothly he felt dizzy. Monster was still subdued, however. Like a dull ache that never went away. Or like a spoiled child.

In the rear-vision mirror he saw the outline of Melanie lying there. Now she was his to keep. Forever. He wondered what dreams pursued her through the dark hours.

At 9.35 a battered Honda Civic pulled up outside the Spence property. Its small engine raced. Mrs

Spence climbed out and waved as the car drove off.

End of another day. She turned to go inside, jumped when she saw a figure approaching down the steep driveway.

'Only me, Mrs Spence. Putting your bin back.'

She relaxed. Reg, her elderly neighbour. A couple of weeks ago some kids saw the bin standing alone on the verge and decided to take it for a ride down one of the laneways. At least they didn't wreck it.

'Sorry if I scared you, Mrs Spence. I should have done it earlier but I just remembered.' The old man stepped into a pool of streetlight. 'That boyfriend is up to his old tricks again. Heard him driving off earlier.'

'Was Melanie with him?'

'Couldn't say. Sorry.'

Brad. How many times had she asked Melanie to have a word with him about his driving? She started up the driveway, fumbling in her bag for the back door key.

'I think you got some mail.' The voice drifted across lawn. 'Noticed it still sitting there after I came back from my walk.'

He was right, of course. She grabbed the bundle of mail. God, hadn't Melanie even bothered to check?

Probably too interested in entertaining Brad. She just hoped the house wasn't in a mess.

But the house was fine. She locked the back door and walked into the kitchen. No mess. She dropped the mail on the bench and switched on the kettle. Nothing exciting. Bills. A newsletter. These days it was the best she could expect.

While the kettle boiled Mrs Spence walked into her bedroom and kicked off her shoes. All she wanted to do was collapse in front of the tv, enjoy a nice cup of tea and salvage what was left of her evening.

On her way back through to the kitchen she paused. Strange, in the passageway she smelled something. Not from the bathroom. She pushed open Melanie's door a fraction and the smell was distinct. What? She hoped it wasn't what she thought it could be. That would be the end. First upper-school tantrums, then Brad, now this. She opened Melanie's window and clean air washed in.

The kettle boiled. She hurried out of Melanie's room and closed the door behind her.

Collie River was wide and slow-moving. He sat in darkness on the bonnet, cross-legged, eyes closed, listening to night song: a screech of water fowl, the distant loping of kangaroos, a cooling breeze cutting through branches. Claudia would have liked this moment. She would have leaned against him, warm and soft by his side.

The take-away chicken was undercooked; he left most of it and ate the chips instead. When he finished those he tossed the box into the river. He produced the back door key, turned it over in his greasy fingers and did the same. He waited for the satisfying *plink*.

Melanie heard nothing, of course. She would sleep for hours yet, until the mixture wore off and her bodily functions returned to normal. In the meantime he would keep an eye on her, occasionally checking her pulse rate and respiration to make sure her temperature did not soar. She was fine when he checked just minutes ago. With any luck he might get a good night's sleep himself.

He hopped down off the bonnet and washed his hands in the river. The water was cold and his skin jumped. His breathing was laboured; he took out the Ventolin inhaler and sucked the shrill song into his lungs. If only he'd been strong, his sister would never have left. But the town hadn't cared. Mumma hadn't cared. The cowboy was dead and sweet Claudia easy pickings. No matter. This time he would be stronger. Melanie would stay by his side forever.

Late again. Twenty-seven minutes to be exact. Hopelessly, Mrs Spence tried to ignore the clock on the video recorder. How many times had she begged Melanie not do this to her? And how many times had Melanie assured her that she wouldn't? Some promise. Ever since she started seeing Brad her promises had turned to dust. Or was it all part of turning sixteen? She hoped not.

She took her empty coffee mug to the kitchen and rinsed it under the hot tap. Now Melanie was thirty-two minutes late and still no sign. On the kitchen wall stood the phone. Naturally. But this time she refused to pick up the receiver. That would would be too much. Why give Melanie the satisfaction of knowing she was *that* worried?

Last time was different. She had surrendered and dialled out. She felt so silly, phoning around to check up on her daughter.

Maybe hot chocolate would relax her. Ten minutes to midnight. She filled the kettle, switched it on and reached up for the hot chocolate canister on the shelf above. As she did the phone rang. She dropped the canister. Swore. Snatched up the receiver.

'Speaking.'

A woman's voice she did not recognise, telling her things she did not want to know. Mrs Spence leaned on the kitchen bench for support and tried to make sense of what she was hearing.

'I've spoken to the girls separately,' continued the voice. 'I'm sure I don't know what got into them. Especially Rachel. Angela I could understand, but Rachel ought to have known better.'

Mrs Spence listened. Her foot trailed in the chocolate powder and she felt her breathing tighten.

'Believe me, Mrs Spence. I feel so bad about this.'

'Melanie wasn't at the social?' Something shifted inside. 'The girls are quite sure about this?'

'That's why I phoned. If I hadn't overheard them talking about it just then.' The voice faded on the line, then: 'You don't think—'

Her throat went dry. 'Look, is there any chance at all that they could have made a mistake, maybe missed Melanie all together?'

'I don't see how. Rachel says they agreed to meet in there. And anyway . . . '

'Yes?'

'Mrs Spence, I don't wish to cause bad blood between you and your daughter, but I overheard the girls talking about a trip to Margaret River. Some sort of surfing event.'

The Surfmasters. She wanted to kick herself for not guessing sooner. Some of the Thursday night casuals had been talking about going straight after work. And Melanie had even mentioned it herself two days ago, only she hadn't really been listening.

'I felt so bad,' said the voice again. 'Neither girl has ever done this kind of thing before.'

'Look, does Rachel know if Melanie planned to go on this trip?'

Another pause, only this time longer. Was that someone whispering in the background? Mrs Spence heard the receiver change hands.

'I'm really sorry, Mrs Spence. Honest. I don't want to get Melanie into trouble.'

Rachel's voice. She sounded nervous.

'It's okay, Rachel. Look, all I want to know is where she is. Did she mention anything at all about going off with Brad?'

'But that's just it. That's what the fight was about. At lunchtime.'

'Brad didn't want her to go?'

'No, the opposite. Brad nagged her to go, but

Melanie kept turning him down. She reckoned she didn't want the hassles.'

Now it was her turn to sound nervous. 'Rachel, listen to me carefully. You're saying you don't think Melanie is with Brad? Is that it?'

'I dunno any more. She sounded like she really meant it. Angela reckons she saw Brad after school but. I was kind of surprised, you know, because Mel sounded so definite she wouldn't be going.'

Slowly a murky picture emerged. Mrs Spence remembered her phone conversation with Melanie. She said she went to the shops to pick up her purse. But suppose she went to buy a few things for the weekend? And hadn't Reg next door heard Brad's car driving off? Okay, so he hadn't actually seen Melanie, but it made sense.

'Mrs Spence, I'm real sorry if me and Angela did something wrong.'

'Don't worry about it. If anyone should be sorry it's Melanie and that no-good boyfriend of hers.'

The conversation ended quickly. She glanced up at the clock. Almost midnight. This time Melanie had gone too far. Way too far.

FRIDAY MORNING

A blindfold, unmistakably real as the strip of fabric pressed against her eyelids. The backwash of memory dumped her and her first instinct was to scream.

Don't.

Instead she listened hard. She heard birds. Lots of birds. Was it early morning or was she some place deep in the bush?

The blindfold prevented Melanie from opening her eyes. More than that, when she went to pull her hand to her face she discovered her wrists were firmly bound behind her back. Ankles, too. Her heels touched hard metal and she pulled away. Was she tied up on some monstrous bed?

Suddenly she was scared. Who was he? What

did he want? She thought of her own father and the fear turned to something else. Distaste? Rage?

Should I tell someone?

He was more than just a harmless creep. On Wednesday she should have stormed into the library, marched up to the loans desk and insisted someone phone the cops. Anything. Too late now. He must have been waiting for the right moment to strike.

If only she hadn't been in such a hurry to try and stop Brad being angry. Some joke. If Brad could see her now he would rip the creep's head off.

More surprises. Everything was a blank past a certain point. She remembered he grabbed her and she lost consciousness. He must have brought her to this room, this bed. What happened next? Insanely, she probed her body to reveal something, anything.

So tell me. Has Brad made it to second base yet?

The shooting pain in her lower back masked everything. How could she even know? She was no expert, not like Rachel or Angela. Sex was something other girls did. That was when the fear returned, gut-wrenching and all-consuming. She wanted to squeeze up into a tight ball and pretend he didn't exist, that this bed wasn't real, that the stories inside her spine were her imagination.

But there was only so much pretending.

Mrs Spence woke with a start and it took a moment to realise where she was. Lounge room. After last night's call she had wandered back here and sat for hours. No tv. No lights. She must have drifted off to sleep.

Across the room the video recorder was a green eye blinking. 6.49 am. Her neck had tensed up and she recognised the crude workings of a migraine. Getting up she moved awkwardly across the room and pulled open the curtains. No noise. Felt cocooned in her own misery. Everything was wrong: the house, Melanie's absence and not even a note or a phone call to say she was all right.

On her way to the kitchen Mrs Spence noticed something on the floor in the passageway. Melanie's necklace. She picked it up, walked into Melanie's room and placed it on the dresser. That was when she noticed that the photo of Melanie and Brad was missing. She pulled open Melanie's top drawer. Nothing. She pulled open the second drawer. Empty. And the bottom drawer was empty. One dress was missing from her wardrobe.

'Melanie?'

She noticed the schoolbag, left untouched in its usual spot. Mrs Spence fell back onto Melanie's bed and leaned forward with her face cupped in her hands. This was more than a weekend away. But the thought was insane. Melanie could never have walked out like that, not after last year and all their troubles.

Outside a magpie hopped across the back lawn and onto the patio. Melanie's window had been left open all night and now the room was chilly. She got up to close it and went to the kitchen. God, the chocolate powder from last night! She stepped round the mess and picked up the phone.

She felt sick. It hurt to swallow. Footsteps approached. A door swung open. He walked over to the bed, pulled down her blindfold and the light exploded. He loosened the knot behind her neck and the strip of cotton fell away.

'Let me go. You have no—'

'Quiet, please, Melanie. I only want to help you.'

She cringed at his touch. His fingertips traced the outline of her nose, smoothed first one cheek then the other. She begged her body not to back away and cause him to explode.

'That's better.' He spoke calmly. 'No one will

hear you if you shout, Melanie. Trust me.'

Trust who? What kind of maniac was she dealing with here?

'Breakfast time.' He rolled the words gently at her. 'I have to untie you. Don't get scared.'

She said nothing. He pulled her round and untied the cords binding her ankles together. Her school skirt rode up and she felt the blood rush into her cheeks. He wore fancy boots.

'It's much easier if you cooperate, Melanie.'

Next he worked on her wrists. The moment passed and she realised she had to say something. Anything.

'You can't treat me like this. It's against—'

'Hush now, sweet child. Did you sleep well?'

'Look, I don't know what game you're playing, but if you don't let me go right now, this very instant—'

'Yes?'

Melanie stopped herself. She sounded corny.

'Well, I'm waiting.'

'I want you to let me go,' she said, softly this time.

'You didn't answer my question. I asked you if you slept well.'

'Look, please. I don't know who you are. I don't care. I just want to go home.'

'I slept well. Slept all night.'

Melanie sucked cool air from the room. Was he a retard?

'You'll have to let me go sooner or later.'

'You think so?'

Eyes wide, she tried to get a good look at him as he finished untying her. No one she knew. When that failed she looked around her. Just an average master bedroom, not that much different in size and taste from her mother's room. At least it wasn't a dark cellar.

'Is it my father? Has he got something to do with this?'

'No. Should he have?'

On the dressing table she saw beads, make-up, a large Garfield grinning back at her like a sick joke.

'I just thought maybe—'

'Your father doesn't live with you anymore, right?'

'I don't want to talk about it. Not him. Not you. Nothing. I just want to be allowed to go home.'

'Stand up.' He hauled her onto her feet.

'Hey!'

'If you're good you'll get Coco Pops.'

And if she was bad? She didn't want to think about that.

* * *

The police car swung into the Spence driveway just after 8.50. Mrs Spence opened the front door and scanned the street. Two teenage boys furiously rode their bikes on their way to school.

'Mrs Spence?'

Both officers looked ridiculously young as they walked over. Mrs Spence fought back her disappointment. It shouldn't matter how young they were as long as they knew their job.

Minutes later, seated in her lounge room, she realised they knew nothing. One took notes while the other asked the kind of ridiculous questions she thought only existed in movies. On the coffee table the necklace was already forgotten as they excavated Brad and Melanie's relationship.

'Look, I've tried to tell you. I hardly know the boy. But I know he's manipulating her.' She eyed the necklace. 'Haven't you listened to a word I've said?'

'Mrs Spence, if we suspected for one moment there was even the slightest hint of foul play.' Quietly spoken, he let the statement hang there, as if to reassure her everything was all right.

'But her clothes,' she repeated, wanting to take them through the house a second time. 'She took just about everything.'

'Yes, everything except her dirty laundry. You said yourself she left her favourite Mambo t-shirt and best pair of Levis.'

'Yes, but—'

'She was in a hurry, Mrs Spence. Rushing around. Makes sense to me.'

She saw his partner eyeing the kitchen behind her. She hadn't cleaned up the chocolate powder and wanted to crawl into the nearest corner.

'*Do* something! She's all I have left since—'

'Mrs Spence, please. There's no use getting upset.'

'I'm not getting upset. I just want to know what's going on.'

'You say your neighbour heard the boyfriend's car drive off?'

She nodded. The officers looked at each other. She wasn't stupid. She knew what they were thinking.

'You don't understand. Melanie isn't the type of girl to just run away like that.'

'Mrs Spence, I don't mean to be rude but if I had a dollar for every time I've heard a parent say that.'

'Fine. Don't believe me. But what if this Brad character does something stupid? He's a bad influence.'

'Mrs Spence, you're just upset.'

'Of course I'm upset! She's only a child.'

The partner leaned forward and picked up the necklace. 'I'm sure your daughter is perfectly safe,' he said, still not looking at her. 'Nine times out of ten it's nothing more than a couple of kids ignoring the consequences of their actions.'

'She's in trouble.' Her voice sounded firm. 'This Brad character. He's not good. He's been in trouble before.'

That got a reaction.

'What kind of trouble?'

She remembered the strange odour last night, dismissed the possibility immediately. 'How should I know! You're the experts!'

'We have to return to the station, Mrs Spence. We'll get in touch.'

'You don't care.' Blood rushed to her cheeks as both officers stood up to leave. 'Something's wrong, I know it is.'

They weren't listening anymore. Melanie was just another runaway. Two minutes later they were gone.

A creep, but what kind of creep? The kind that watches you eat breakfast without saying a word. The kind that stands guard outside the bathroom while you shower and change into jeans and a t-shirt. It was the fastest shower she could ever remember.

'Feeling better?'

'Yes.' She practically spat the word at him.

'Good. I don't want you to be scared of me, Melanie. I only want what's best for both of us.'

'Look, if you let me go I won't tell the police anything. I promise.'

'You've been watching too many videos, Melanie.'

'I mean it. I'll make up a story. Say I got depressed and slept in the park. Anything. The police don't have to know.'

'Enough. Don't push it.'

'But you're not even listening—'

'Shut it, I said!'

He wasn't fooling. Melanie sensed his rage and kept her mouth shut. Tight.

He led her back to the bedroom and closed the door behind her. She did not want to think about the rest. But she couldn't stop thinking. Through a mist she remembered the cotton swab. He was too strong for her as his poison scratched and clawed her nostrils and throat, burning her eyes. And then what?

Nothing.

Some kind of drug?

Probably. That would explain the nausea still spiralling loose inside. She hated him already, hated the predictability of him. Why did so many men have to wear their strength like a badge? Surely they didn't really believe in all that macho bullshit!

He left her untied. No blindfold. She was free, but only after she promised to stay on the bed and she wouldn't make a sound.

Don't disappoint me. I hate to be disappointed.

Melanie swung her legs over the edge of the bed and stood up. Dizzy. Some small point inside her head shifted uneasily to migraine. She located the pain stored behind her eyeballs and groaned softly. Screw his disappointment. She couldn't just sit there, doing nothing. There had to be a way out of this nightmare.

Maybe there was. If she cooperated fully he might feel sorry for her and let her go. Hadn't that maniac over in Sydney let his victims go? Victims. Such an ugly word. Weren't the Jews victims, crowded into freight cars and unloaded at Auschwitz extermination camp, always fighting for every piece of bread and hoping someone else might die in their place.?

No, she could never cooperate fully. Since she had no choice, she decided to play his depraved little game by her own rules, not his, always looking and waiting for her chance to beat him.

Starting right now.

Two possible exits: the door, which would be locked, and a window of orange rage. Melanie felt warm sunlight sluice through the thin fabric. Her bare feet scuffed on the carpet. Still dizzy, she reached the cheap curtains and hesitated. What if he was out there, relishing this very moment?

But the window provided a chance. That was important. She eased back the curtain, just a fraction, and her disappointment was immediate. No known landmark greeted her, just an enclosed wooden fence edging onto lawn. A small garage occupied the top corner of the garden, its roller door drawn down like a large eye winking. Behind the fence she saw suburban roofs and a series of tall gums stuck onto sky. Any fence. Everyone's sky.

Moving to the other side, Melanie again pulled the curtain aside. She cried out, and immediately wished she hadn't.

He dropped the newspaper he was reading, turned and looked directly at her. Melanie leapt forward, around the bed, and with both hands she turned the door knob. What if he got angry, really angry, enough to seriously hurt her? God, he might even kill her. Men were capable of anything.

'Please! Somebody! Anybody!'

Something gave. The door swung open onto a central passageway.

One door to her left. Two doors and a gaping archway to her right. Directly ahead the front door. Escape!

Out back Melanie heard the *clang* of an aluminium flyscreen and heavy footsteps approaching. He whistled a cheerful tune! Probably coming through the laundry, now the kitchen.

Run! Go! Smash straight through the front door if need be.

The tiny girl was suddenly there, stepping into the passageway and blocking her escape. She clutched a large pink elephant. She had been crying; her tears had carved a dry creek bed down each cheek.

Behind Melanie a door swung open and rough hands grabbed her around the waist.

'No! You can't do this to me!

His whistling stopped. She didn't want him

anywhere near her. Even as his hand clamped onto her mouth and his other hand grabbed her hard, fingers digging deep into her shoulder blades, she kicked, struggled, tried to spin around and scratch out his eyes.

The small girl watched it all.

QUESTIONS

'Don't worry about making a mess.' Brad threw his sleeping bag into the back seat, along with the rest of his gear. 'Just chuck it in.'

'Hope you don't mind.' His new girlfriend stepped back from the car and walked over to the dying camp fire. Now that the sun had risen above the tops of the trees there was no need to seek the glowing embers.

He shrugged his shoulders. 'I don't mind.'

'It's just that they put me on the noon shift so that I could have tonight and tomorrow night free.'

'It's okay.' The way she stood there, her long blonde hair falling past her shoulders and down to her waist. How could he mind?

She winked. 'We don't have to be back in

Bunbury for three hours yet.'

'Come here.' He stumbled after her, across the open ground, past the cars, tents, dripping wetsuits left to dry on gum tree branches.

She laughed, spun round in a wide circle. Across the field two large kangaroos picked up speed and were lost in the thick scrub. An old Holden ute, stacked high with surfboards and Eskys, bashed its way out of Contos camping grounds and headed back to Caves Road for the short drive into town.

'Yo, Brad-ley! Nice party, man!' One of his feral mates surfaced from behind the bush, a first tinny well under way. 'Heard you're leaving us already.'

'Nah.' He pointed to the girlfriend, already some distance along the beach track. 'Needs a lift back to Bunbury. I'll be back tonight.'

His mate laughed. 'But Bunbury's the other way!'

Brad nodded. 'Yeah, but first she needs something else.'

Early afternoon. Monster was greedy to get going. It detested being strapped to Ashmere like this, like some dangerous zoo animal anaesthetised. And deep down Samuel Levine knew Monster was right. Staying only dulled the senses. They could never stay and be safe. Too dangerous. A week might arouse unwelcome scrutiny. A fortnight would guarantee unwanted questions. The last thing he needed was the neighbourhood leaning over his shoulder in judgment, curious to see who he was and what he was up to.

So often he was judged, sentenced, taken out into the yard and pinned against the wall. Some held him while others put the boot in, knocked his teeth out, smashed his face against the brick work. How many times had they left him there, body broken and bloodied on the hard bitumen?

And everyone laughed to see such fun.

No matter. Soon his family would be complete. Once they reached Darwin it would be a simple matter of stealing a boat. In Indonesia there were thousands of islands to escape to, many only a couple of kilometres long. He could be Captain Kidd, pirate prince and scourge of the southern seas. Pirates were a bit like cowboys. They would take their booty up into the jungle mountains and spit in the eye of creation. His girls would care for him, never condemn him. In return he would love them and give them the happiness they longed for.

Something in the atmosphere of the house changed

and Melanie got frightened. The girl sobbed loudly. It got under her skin. Who was she?

It was impossible for Melanie to offer any comfort. After her attempt to escape, the creep threw her on the bed, tied her back up and placed the blindfold back on. He said he was very disappointed in her attitude. She would never forget the humiliation of hearing him lecture her like that. He sounded just like Brad, which worried her. Maybe it was that macho thing again. Boys liked to tell big ones. And girls loved to believe them.

She heard something. The door slowly swung open and was left ajar. With her eyes bandaged shut against the day it was impossible to say who, but she hoped it was the girl. Twice now she had heard the door swing open, heard the patter of bare feet, felt the small hands on her face, touching her nose and cheeks before quickly walking away.

But it wasn't the girl. Once more she heard his voice, felt his strong man's touch. She wanted to squirm away. His fingers were poison.

'Time to eat. Then I want you to have an afternoon nap.'

He didn't remove her blindfold. He didn't even untie her wrists. Gutless, just like her father with his awful toys. Did it turn him on, make him hard, send his pulse racing?

'Here. Sit up.' He yanked her forward and roughly pulled her up into a sitting position.

'Look, I'm sorry. I didn't—'

'No talking, Melanie. Remember our contract. No nothing until you learn to obey.'

She tried to sit forward, to ease the weight pressing back on her shoulders. With her arms behind her back it was an awkward position. God, she despised him already. Despised everything he stood for. Wished she could tell him where to get off.

'After you've eaten I'll let you go to the toilet. I might be late getting back.'

'Back?'

'No talking, Melanie!'

He was going somewhere. Would he take the girl?

'Now, eat.' One hand lifted up her chin while the other pushed something gently against her lips. A Vegemite roll. Great. She hated Vegemite. Slowly, she took a first bite.

The siren. School finished for another week. Rachel should have felt glad. She felt lousy. As soon as they got home Mum would be waiting to take her and Angela in to Bunbury to help her with the groceries. Boring.

'Rachel!'

She turned round and saw Mrs Spence heading through the bike racks. She smiled, then wondered if that was the right thing to do. None of her friends had ever run away before.

Mrs Spence looked awful as she approached. 'Rachel, can I talk to you for a moment?'

'Sure.'

'About Melanie and this Brad character?'

She nodded quickly. 'Anything you say.'

'Do you know where they might have gone together?'

'No. Mrs Spence, you've got believe me—'

'I don't know who to believe anymore. You kids. You all stick together.'

Rachel was shocked. Up close Melanie's mother looked worse than awful. Clearly she had not been to work. Nearby, a couple of girls stopped talking and stared. It was embarrassing.

No one saw him ditch the credit card. He dropped it into an empty chip packet, crumpled the packet up in his fist and threw it into the rubbish bin outside the

Commonwealth Bank. Chances were it would never be found. Tonight the rubbish bin would be emptied into one large dump bin out back. And soon a garbage truck would arrive, early one morning or late one evening, and maybe the driver would dream about getting a better job as he loaded up his stinking core of noise. That easy. In a country the size of Australia you could hide just about anything.

'Let's drive in to Bunbury.' He needed to hunt through the bookshops and buy a traveller's guide to Indonesia. Something comprehensive. 'If you're good I'll buy you a toy at the Singing Tree.'

The girl looked up at him, said nothing. No matter. After the bookshops he would drive out to Pizza Hut and buy the works. Life on the run made for a hungry tummy.

As they headed back across the car park, Levine saw someone leaning over the windscreen of the panel van. He stopped and stared, half-hidden behind a Toyota Tarago. He pulled the girl in close.

The woman was in her twenties, plainly dressed with just a hint of a weight problem showing through. She placed a scrap of paper under the windscreen wiper and walked away. He watched her climb into a late-model hatchback, waited for her to drive out of the car park and out of sight.

When they reached the panel van he scanned the car park, looking for occupied cars. Nothing. He snatched up the message.

Missed you at aqua-aerobics this week. Did you forget? Will phone you tonight. PS See you at Hungry Jacks tomorrow.

Hungry Jacks. That would explain the party invitation on the fridge back at the house.

'You know that lady?'

The girl nodded.

'A friend of your mummy?'

She looked at the ground.

'I see.' He tore up the message and threw it at her small feet. No, Mummy hadn't forgotten aqua-aerobics. She just wasn't able to go, that was all. Monster had talked her out of it. Monster had a way with words.

I want you to have an afternoon nap.

Who was he kidding? When she was a kid and she couldn't sleep Melanie played a game at night to see how long she could swim under the blankets without breathing. One time she made it fourteen lengths before the blood pounding at her temple forced her to kick off the covers and suck new air from the darkness. One time the ice cracked and the fur trader sank straight to the bottom of the frozen lake, and right away the lake covered over because it was so cold. Melanie remembered the story her teacher had told. She linked it to her childhood game. Only this time the game was real. The creep would never let go. He would hold her here in this murky secret room forever. Ice melts, but cords and blindfolds hold real tight. That's the way he would keep her, by shutting her away from the light. And that's why he had left the tv on, loud and hysterical, somewhere else in the house.

No one will hear you shout, Melanie.

Clever. Very clever. Someone ought to make him a hero. Or punch his lights out. Was it a sin to think such evil thoughts? Tough. He started it.

Minutes ago she had heard the school siren again. A couple of sirens. Wherever she was, there were schools. Schools meant safety. All she needed to do was make a run for it now that she had the house to herself. Or did she? The girl had been a complete surprise. What if she was still out there, his very own spy? Impossible. But what if he had an accomplice, someone bigger, meaner, more violent?

Great.

No, that was bulldust! The creep was on his

own. Even if he wasn't, she couldn't just stay here and do nothing. She wasn't some scared little kiddie with no place to run. Not now. Not ever. There had to be a way out.

Lying on her side, she slowly shifted her weight across the bed until her face and knees hovered over the edge. She swung her feet out onto the carpet and pulled herself up into a sitting position. There. Now she was on the edge of the bed and faced the window. She tried to ignore the blindfold and re-create the room from memory. The door was to her left, no more than two metres beyond the end of the bed. Any furniture? Only the dressing-table on the far side.

Satisfied, she stood up and inched her way along the edge of the bed, using her heels and fingertips as a guide until she reached the end. Easy. She kept going, across the carpet, feeling her whole body tense up along the way. What if she fell? She did not fall, however. Her left shoulder grazed the wall and she turned round until her hands and heels once again served as a guide. Real easy. Wall plaster gave way to a wooden surface. Moments later her shoulder blade found the doorknob. Cold. Beautiful.

She leaned forward, stretching up on her toes to

reach the doorknob behind her. Almost. Almost reaching. Yes! She turned it all the way until she heard its welcome *click*. Pulled. Hard. Harder. The door did not budge.

'No!'

She let go. Relaxed, then tried again. This time she yanked hard, almost dislocating her shoulder in the process. Still no good. He must have done something on the other side.

'Let me go! Now!'

All she heard was the loud tv, mocking her back to silence.

'Please! Someone! Anyone!'

Real life wasn't like in the movies. It wasn't some Plains Video weekly special. It wanted to suffocate her.

THAT'S ENTERTAINMENT

On the way back from Bunbury he stopped off at the Ashmere BP service station. In the driveway sat a rusty old Kingswood sedan. He pulled up alongside a second pump and reached behind for the empty jerry can. He turned to the girl.

'You stay in the car now. I'll get you a Coke.'

'But I like lemonade.'

'Tough. You'll get what you're given.'

The girl stared ahead. She hadn't touched her magic glitter wand. No matter. In the weeks to come she would learn to appreciate the presents he bought her.

On the rear seat of the Kingswood sat two teenage girls with their backs to him. He ignored them. First he filled the petrol tank. The numbers spun in the steel jacket of the pump and he managed to squeeze in one more dollar before petrol bubbled up past the lip and down the side of the panel van. He pulled out the nozzle, replaced the petrol cap, swung round to the jerry can and started to fill it. When he was finished he placed the jerry can back in the panel van.

Inside the service station Levine kept his head down. He found the soft drinks fridge and made his selection. The woman behind the cash register took his money and handed over his change without paying him much attention.

Good.

The owner of the Kingswood passed him on the driveway.

'Hey, Mum! Can we have a packet of chips? We're both starving!'

He heard the woman sigh.

'Please, Mum!'

Levine recognised the girl's face as she leaned out the back window of the Kingswood. Melanie's friend. Both friends! He hurried to the panel van.

'Here.' He handed the girl her can of Coke as he sat behind the wheel and waited to get going. In the service station he saw the woman carry two packets of chips to the counter.

Beside him the girl went to open the door and his hand flashed across the seat to grab her wrist hard. She cried out. He knocked the magic glitter wand to the floor by her feet.

'Don't!' he hissed. 'You're with me now!'

Monster was not content simply to ride out the storm. No, monster wanted to move, to act, to punch out. Monster's impatience swelled to anger, started to twist slowly, slowly, a funnel of rage. He had to get away, drive away, get the hell out of there, dammit. Just like when Mumma's screams tried to knock him down.

At last! The mother returned and got into the Kingswood. The car started up. Levine relaxed his grip and the girl pulled her hand free. She started to cry.

'It's nothing.' His voice sounded cracked. 'Drink your Coke.'

The Kingswood was going now. For a moment he watched the car turn out of the service station and onto the road. Everything was fine.

How many hours passed before Melanie heard the vehicle pull up alongside the house and the car door slam? Three? Four? Even the school sirens had finished for the week.

Once inside he turned the volume down on the tv, brought her some pizza and fed her. She ate greedily, finished a second generous slice as she fought back her revulsion. To be hand-fed like this, blindfold still in place, made her want to puke. But she ate anyway. Was this how prisoners felt?

'Did you have your afternoon nap?'

She nodded. Lied.

'Good. Tomorrow's going to be a long day.'

She wanted to say something but remembered his stupid rule. Fine. Be a turd. It could wait until morning. She finished eating and he left the room, closing the door behind him.

How many more hours passed? She thought she heard the signature tune for the channel seven evening news. Or was that the late evening update? She couldn't tell anymore.

The phone rang, continued ringing until whoever it was gave up. That was the third time now and she wondered why he refused to pick up the receiver.

The bedroom door opened. A sitcom laughed at its own jokes. The door closed and Melanie sensed the swirl of movement beside the bed. Every nerve seemed to yell out to her. Even though she wanted to, she was unable to move her body away. But then she felt the small weight climbing up onto the bed next to her and she relaxed.

Small fingers dug at the knot behind her head. The blindfold fell away and Melanie discovered the room in darkness.

'Hi.' She couldn't make out the girl's features even though she sat right next to her on the bed. She almost didn't see the raised cup in time. 'Thank you.' She took a small drink of water, drank some more. Pizza made you thirsty.

'Who are you?'

The girl didn't answer.

Melanie thought about her wrists and ankles, still securely bound. This was her punishment. He said she would spend all day and night tied up and he meant it. He also said he might untie her after breakfast tomorrow if she promised not to be silly. Really generous. If only she could win the small girl's trust. But the girl took the cup of water out of her hands and climbed back down off the bed. She sniffed loudly. Had she been crying?

'No. wait.' Melanie worked on appearing calm. This morning, when she had struggled in his arms, she saw the puzzled look the girl gave.

Now the girl listened.

'I didn't mean to scare you.'

Still listening.

'I wanted to get away. He's a bad man. We have to get away.'

'No.' She sniffed again.

'Yes! Look, I don't know who you are, but I know we're both in big trouble.' Her voice dropped to a whisper. 'He dragged me from my home. He even knew my name.'

The words seemed to wash over the girl. She stood there in the dark and it was impossible to see her face, let alone tell what she was thinking. She was upset, though.

'Monster hurt Mummy.'

The statement stunned Melanie. Had she heard correctly? She shifted uncomfortably on the bed, her back aching after so many hours in the propped-up position.

'Hurt Mummy bad.'

Something jarred. Suddenly the girl was moving back towards the door.

'No, wait!' How could she run away like that? 'Stay and talk. Tell me who you are.'

The girl moved quickly to the door and opened it.

'Let me help you.'

But the girl was gone, closing the door behind her.

* * *

Angela sat on the sofa, flicking through the tv guide. 'I heard some girls talking about Margaret River.' She didn't bother to look up.

Rachel sat at the dining table, her face buried in homework. She stopped writing. 'What girls?'

'Dunno. Overheard one of them saying her older brother's been staying down there for the Surfmasters.'

'And?'

Angela turned the magazine round to face her sister. 'Nice buns. D'ya reckon he'd be looking for a new girlfriend?'

'Angela!'

'Oh, yeah. The older brother. Sounded like Contos camping grounds went right off last night.'

Rachel hoped her oldies stayed in the kitchen. She put down her pen and closed her file. 'Look, did these girls say anything else? I need to know.'

Angela threw down the tv guide. 'I better get Mum and Dad. Their show starts in two minutes.'

'Fine. Don't tell me.'

Angela stood up, smoothing her skirt as she walked over to the dining table. 'Everyone's having a good time. One of the mob got arrested for abusive language. Someone fired a shotgun.

Two tents burned down and a ute got rolled.'

'What about Melanie and Brad?'

'Never heard anything about Melanie. Brad must have a new girlfriend but. That girl who works over at Plains Video.'

'You're joking!'

'Don't you want to know which surfers made it through?'

'Angela, please.'

'Just as well.' Angela walked away. ''Cos it sounded like everyone was too stoned to care.'

She was asleep. He woke her. The girl hadn't replaced Melanie's blindfold earlier and now there was no mistaking her confusion as she blinked back the light washing into the bedroom.

'It's okay, Melanie. Relax.'

But she didn't relax. She kicked hard like she wanted to hurt him and screamed loud like she wanted to wake the whole sleeping world. So futile. But he didn't want her waking the girl. She was young and needed her sleep. It made her easier to handle.

One hand flew to her shoulder, the other onto her mouth and he rode out her useless struggles. Her eyes registered a different emotion now. No matter. She would learn. He held her down until she got the message.

'There. That's better.' She stopped being silly and he took his hands away. 'All I wanted was to make you more comfortable.'

She nodded, staring up at him.

'Here. Sit up.'

Now Melanie cooperated and he was glad.

'I have a special treat for you.'

Again, she nodded. He pulled back the bed covers, moved down to her ankles and untied the cords binding her feet. He stood her up. She wore the same jeans and t-shirt from this morning. Tomorrow, when he sent her to the bathroom, he would issue a fresh change of clothes. She mustn't think he was uncivilised.

'Let's go, Melanie.' He led her slowly along the bright passageway and she almost tripped.

'Sorry,' she said quickly.

'It's okay. Through there.' He steered her through the open doorway of the front room and sat her down on the sofa. The tv was soft snow. Before waking her he had turned the sound down, along with the lights. He liked the cinematic feel.

'You like movies?' he asked.

She nodded.

'Me too. Westerns mainly. In westerns the good guy always wins.'

She said nothing.

'My daddy was a good guy, but he lost anyway. It was all Mumma's fault. Mumma never loved him. She never loved anyone but herself. Not me. Not Claudia. She can't hurt me now.'

'Please—'

'I know. I talk too much. Let's watch the video instead.'

Melanie sat there, on the edge of the sofa, and he sat down beside her. He raised the remote control, aimed at the video recorder, and pressed play. Something clicked inside the machine.

Years ago, the night Mumma died, he drove into Geraldton to catch the double feature at the Highway Drive-in. He knew the police were out looking for him. Beneath the darkening sky, shirt unbuttoned to collect the cooling breeze, he watched giant lips move. In those days he took in movies with titles like *Midnight Cowboy*, one-of-a-kind movies made before mechanical sharks and steroids blasted the industry part. Cowboy stories were better than medication.

A woman arrived on her own. She drove a red convertible sports car. He watched her chrome bumper inch forward, heard the crunch of gravel as she straightened her wheels. As she reached out and took the speaker he breathed in her perfume. She sat close by, safe inside her skin of metal and red duco. To be that close to a female, to sense the rivers of blood flowing through her body, yet never know her name or catch her eye or even acknowledge her presence. That was the modern disease. So he whispered to her. The woman glanced sideways, quickly returned the speaker to its post and drove away. He watched the brake lights several bays on. After that he couldn't breathe properly. The drive-in screen leaned over him like a slow interrogation. Twenty minutes later he had sat handcuffed in Geraldton Police Station.

But why spoil tonight's offering? The snow blacked out and he pulled Melanie close. Her body stiffened as the screen brightened.

'Relax. I saved it 'specially for you.' He placed his arm around her shoulders, leaned back into the sofa and got comfortable. She kept her hands on her knees and started to cry.

'What's wrong?'

'Please. Not this. Now now.'

The screen filled with washed colour; the room filled with soft music. A naked couple stepped in front of the camera, embraced, kissed hungrily. The camera panned more couples, some standing, some reclining, everyone naked.

'But it's yours, isn't it?' Samuel Levine watched for Melanie's response. 'I found it in your room.'

'Yes, but—'

'You like this stuff?'

She said nothing.

'Your boyfriend likes this stuff?'

'No, you don't understand. It's not my—'

'Tell me about your boyfriend, Melanie. Is he a good guy?'

'Look—'

'I didn't think so. Good guys don't go in for this stuff.'

'It's not Brad's video! It was my father's. He had a whole wardrobe . . .'

She couldn't continue. She tried to block out the screen, the memories. He pulled her hands back down.

'Tell me about your father, Melanie.'

'I already told you. I don't want to talk about him.'

'Did he touch you?'

'God, no. Look, I really—'

'He wanted to touch you?'

'Please.'

'What was in the wardrobe, Melanie?'

'Please, I don't want to—'

'Not just videos? Other stuff?'

'It's none of your business.'

'Magazines? Mail order catalogues? Maybe something worse?'

'Yes! All kinds of things. Now can we change the subject?'

'He scared you, didn't he, Melanie?'

'Look, my father was sick. He made me feel sick. Now can you just leave me alone?'

'Always watching you. Staring at you with his big eyes.'

She started to cry.

'There, there. Shush now, Melanie.'

He leaned into her, his arm still around her shoulders and his hand squeezing the top of her arm.

'I'll protect you,' he said. 'It won't be like before. Mumma's dead. The boys have all moved on. I can be strong for both of us. You'll see.'

'I don't know what you're talking about.'

'Us, Melanie. You, me, Claudia. Oh, and the girl if she decides to be good.'

'Who is Claudia? Is she a girl like me?'

'Yes, Exactly like you.'

'Are there any others?'

'No. Hush now, Melanie. It's getting interesting.'

Again her hands moved up to her face.

'Don't you even want to know how it ends?' he asked.

SATURDAY MORNING

The girl walked through the kitchen and into the dining room, slowly sipping milk from a clear plastic tumbler. Eyes wide, she stood facing Melanie from a small distance. She looked so young, impressionable. Had he succeeded in brainwashing her?

Melanie tried to speak. Impossible. Her muffled pleas made the girl take a step backwards and she immediately stopped.

'Where's my mummy gone?'

Now it was Melanie's turn to be wide-eyed.

'I don't drink milk anymore. Mummy gives me juice.'

If only she could talk. Everything was a big game to him. Like last night, the video. He had made her sit through every frame. So sick to be sitting there, unable to move, hating the feel of his hand on her arm. How could he have guessed so much about her? And afterwards, the way he insisted she go to the toilet before lights out. He hadn't even untied her wrists. Such a low life. Had he listened through the door. Somehow she'd forced herself to go. It had been like peeing in public.

She thought of the girl and felt sick. Did he listen to her, too? Maybe he went further. He fed her. Did he bath her, dress her? She hoped not. No wonder her mother hated men.

Moments ago she had heard him driving the car past the house and into the back garden. She twisted her head back, and the view from the dining-room window confirmed what she already knew. White panel van. Definitely the creep from the shopping centre. No wonder he stared as he drove past.

Melanie sat upright, firmly tied to the kitchen chair. She had her back to the wall. He had carried her out of the bedroom and placed her here, in the dining room, at the kitchen table, a grotesque parody of everyday living. Her wrists and ankles were bound together. She had watched as he looped a length of cord up through the base of the chair and round her waist, her spine, her waist, pulling so tight she was sure her rib cage would crack before he got the knots in place.

Wait!

The girl turned to walk away when she saw Melanie could be no help.

No!

Melanie threw herself back in the chair, her head hitting the wall with sickening force. For a moment her world threatened to topple sideways, to spin out of control and send her and the chair crash-diving to the slate tile floor.

The girl placed her drink on the floor and walked over. Without saying a word she dug her fingers into the gag and pulled the twisted length of cotton loose and finally past Melanie's chin.

'I want Mummy back.'

Melanie glanced sideways through the window. The bonnet was up and the creep leaned over the engine. She saw he had his back to the house, to them.

'I want—'

'Listen to me!'

The girl backed away and for one horrible moment Melanie thought she had blown it.

'No, wait.' She concentrated on speaking softly, gently. 'I'll get you some juice but first you'll have to help me.'

The girl nodded, but made no attempt to move.

'I'm stuck.'

Still no attempt.

'See, I can't move my hands.' She nodded sideways until the girl followed her gaze down the back of the chair to where her wrists were bound. 'That's right. I need your help.'

'Stuck.'

'Yes, I need your help to get me unstuck.'

'Make Mummy come back. It's not fair.'

'Look, can you undo knots?'

The girl looked at Melanie's wrists and shook her head. 'I don't know how.' She seemed puzzled by the request.

'It's easy.' Yet even as she spoke the words Melanie knew it was far from easy, that it was impossible. There was no way the knots were coming off. Deep down inside, in the place where there's no fooling around, she knew she was beaten.

Never!

Outside he was busy. She couldn't let the chance slip by. But what? How?

Top hose, dammit. Levine saw the telltale scar of brown rust started at the radiator lug but ran only as far as the clamp. He bent over the engine block and probed the hose with a long screwdriver.

There!

Not a problem. A small split, that was all. All it needed was a wider clamp. He would race down to the garage and grab one right away. He checked the water level in the radiator. Down only a fraction. See. He filled it back up. The oil level was fine. Overall the motor looked to be in good shape, a comforting thought given the long haul ahead.

When he was finished he grabbed a piece of rag from the tool box and started to wipe his hands. Better take the girl, just in case. Melanie could stay. They wouldn't be gone more than five minutes.

No need to panic.

That other car, the stolen Camry sedan, had got him from Melbourne to South Australia, then on to Norseman and the southern wonders of Western Australia: Esperance, Albany, following the coast then kicking up through the tall timber country before finally hitting Bunbury. Now the Ford panel van would allow him to finish the journey: Bunbury to Perth, then first stop Ellendale Flats, where they would camp by the ocean and look at the stars.

See the stars, Claudia? See how brightly they burn?

What next? Carnarvon, Karratha, Port Hedland, Broome and beyond. He'd punctuate the long hours at the wheel with nightly rest stops along the way. Even the cowboy needed his sleep.

'I'm going to a party at Hungry Jacks.' She turned and pointed to the fridge door. 'Mummy said.'

The girl couldn't be more than four. How did four years olds think?

'Mummy said—'

'Would you like to talk to Mummy?'

She nodded.

'How about right now?'

'Monster took Mummy away.'

Melanie swallowed hard. 'We can bring Mummy back. See the phone over there?'

Up on the breakfast bar sat the phone. The girl nodded without looking.

'Do you know how it works?'

'I think so.'

'Want to try?'

'Mummy said I mustn't play with the phone.'

'Ah, but this won't be playing. This will be real. To Mummy.' She watched the little girl's face brighten. 'Wanna try?'

'Yes, please.'

Was he still out there, working on the car? Melanie quickly looked. She breathed out.

The girl's face shone as she stepped up to the breakfast bar.

'Right. First we pick up the receiver.' The easy part. Melanie kept calm but inside she felt her stomach somersault.

The girl lifted the receiver and pressed it to her ear.

'That's the way.'

'It's making a funny noise.'

'That's right. Now—' Melanie sucked in her breath. The hard part. 'Do you know what number a zero is?'

She shook her head.

'A nought? Nothing?'

Again, she shook her head.

'It's the round one. You know, like a ball.'

'This one!' She pointed.

'Yes. Good. Now I want you to carefully press the button three times. Press it once.'

The small finger hovered, pressed.

'Okay, and again.'

This time there was no hesitation.

'Good. Now one more time.'

The girl pressed, smiled.

Melanie was about to praise her when she heard the bonnet slam down.

'It's ringing!'

'Quickly. Bring it here.'

'But you said—'

'Hurry!'

The girl hesitated. 'Will Mummy be there?'

'Yes!'

The girl pulled the receiver as far as it would reach, a full metre from where Melanie sat.

'Good girl!' She just hoped the dial tone had turned into a woman's voice. Too bad if it hadn't. 'Police! Get me the police!'

He no longer leaned over the engine and she thought she would throw up when she watched him turn round and look directly at the house, both hands buried inside the swirl of rag. He stepped round the front end to the driver's side and fell behind the steering wheel.

'There's a lady on the phone. She's talking.'

The panel van roared into life and he reversed it slowly out of view.

'Hold the phone up!'

The girl did as she was told. Her expression changed, seemed to shift to suspicion, then to fear.

The motor stopped. Melanie heard the car door slam.

'You said—'

'Please! This is not a hoax call! My name is Melanie Spence!' Her mind scrambled over what to say. 'There's this man, see! He's holding me prisoner! Not just—'

Suddenly he was there, rounding the side of the house, passing the dining room window, opening the back flyscreen and entering the house.

'Oh, God. He's coming! Put the phone back! Quickly!'

Not quickly enough. His height seemed to fill the doorway as he looked, saw.

'I want Mummy.'

'Bad! Bad!' He ignored the girl, snatched the receiver out of her hand and sent it crashing into the breakfast bar. Still not satisfied, he rushed over and yanked the phone cord out of the wall.

Melanie screamed at the girl to run, hide. She did not move.

'Shut up!' He spun round, shaking the end of the cord in his fist. 'Do you want Monster to hurt you? Kill you?'

'Let us go!'

'I said shut up! How can I protect you if you

don't cooperate?'

Melanie twisted round to face him. 'I phoned the police!'

'Impossible!'

'They've traced the call and they're on their way!'

Did he believe her? Maybe.

'You can still get away in time.' Her voice, so shaky. 'Go on. Get away!'

'Shut up! Let me think, dammit!'

'Go! Now! They'll be here any second.'

'No, we're family. Families have to stick together.'

'We're not family! You're just some retard who—'

He rushed across the room and slapped her. Hard.

'You can't hit me, you wanker!'

The girl burst into tears. 'You said I could talk to Mummy!' She ran through the kitchen and out of sight. It seemed to jolt him back.

'Oh, dear. Now you've upset her. And just when we were all getting along so nicely.'

'Let us go!' Defiant now, because defiance was all Melanie had left.

'And you've made a mess.' He pointed to the floor, to a spreading pool of milk. 'No matter. We're leaving.'

She stared at him through her tears and he noticed.

'We won't be coming back, Melanie. Not today. Not ever.'

PART TWO

'What sort of man was he?'

'He was a bad man.'

A seven-year-old girl to reporters, after she ran away from a stranger offering her lollies.

TAKEN

Beverley Cruz recognised the shoes immediately. Black wing tips with brown leather laces. Detective Senior Constable Patrick Warren, fifty-four, of the Victoria Police Department, took a half-step back from the side of the health club pool. He towered over her, as he towered over everyone.

'You make it look like hard work.' His hands were tucked inside his long overcoat. He exuded style, but little personality.

'It *is* hard work.' Beverley welcomed the opportunity to rest. 'But it keeps me sane.'

'Something came up. I'll meet you outside.'

'What kind of something?'

'It's cold out. I hope you brought something warm.'

He moved away, his tall thin body cutting a path through the swirls of steam. Beyond the glass cocoon of warm water Beverley saw her boss hunch up his collar against the crisp stillness of a Kosciusko summer.

When she hurried out to him seven minutes later she noticed he sat in the passenger seat of the hire car, blanketed against the cold. Beverley tapped the window and he opened his eyes and nodded.

She walked around to the driver's side. Underfoot a skin of ice cracked like small hulls converging.

'It's Samuel Levine. He's abducted two girls.'

Beverley dropped her sports bag onto the back seat. Goodbye scenery. So long conference.

'One's sixteen. The other's four. No relation.'

They took the shortest route back to the hotel and stayed under the speed limit. She could imagine the stories if she got picked up for speeding en route to an international crime conference.

'He's in Western Australia.' Patrick rested his eyes once more. 'We're booked on the next available flight.'

'Anyone in the field we know?'

'Leo Gwyter will meet us there. He's in charge until we arrive.'

Little more was said. Beverley's morning swim ended in a sickening lurch.

The steam of forty kilometres took the white panel van into Cataby Roadhouse, two hours north of Perth and four hours from Ashmere.

'Be good.' Levine's voice registered no emotion but he knew the girl got his meaning. 'Remember our little talk?'

'I need to go to the toilet.'

'Later,' he snapped. 'Don't make a mess. And don't start crying or Monster will come.'

She didn't start crying.

Cataby Roadhouse was busy: eight vehicles lined up on the driveway for petrol. A tall thin youth eyed him and the girl. He yelled something across the driveway to someone inside the workshop area. A large man in dirty blue overalls stepped into view.

'You've got problems, fella.' The mechanic came across, wiping his hands on an oily rag. 'Losing a lot of cool.'

Levine gripped the steering wheel. The mechanic motioned for him to release the bonnet catch.

'Sure. Of course.' He yanked the release and

stepped out into the dry heat. 'Just borrowed the van from my brother.'

The mechanic stepped back, smiling at the girl. She didn't smile back, merely held up her pink elephant for him to see. Melanie was in the back of the panel van, kept well-hidden behind the closed curtain.

A cloud of steam escaped as Levine lifted up the bonnet. Together he and the mechanic studied the motor. If it hadn't been for Melanie and her phone call there wouldn't be any problem.

'You timed that well.' The split in the top radiator hose sprayed a fine mist of water up onto the motor. 'Soon as she's cooled off a bit I'll whip her off and put a new one on.'

The mechanic headed back to the workshop for a spare.

'No, wait! I'm in a hurry.' Levine knew it must sound suspect. 'What I mean is, I don't want to waste your time. I'll just buy the hose and pull off the road at the next rest area.'

'Suit yourself, mate. Whatever you want.'

Levine followed him back to the workshop. He scanned the restaurant section busy with thirsty, hungry customers. Lunchtime. Everyone chose his or her favourite poison.

'Here you go, mate. Some coolant and two radiator hoses to go.' The mechanic winked. 'Trust me. They always go in pairs.'

The first available flight to Perth would not touch down until just after 3.15. At least Leo Gwyter was on the case.

'So what happened?' Beverley Cruz sat forward in her seat and dismissed the scraps of cloud suspended beneath the wing tip.

'Two weeks ago Levine hired a Camry sedan in Melbourne and didn't return it.' Patrick Warren took off his reading glasses and pushed the paperwork away. 'This morning Bunbury CIB responded to an emergency call. They located the car inside the garage at the back of a property. They also found the four-year-old's mother.'

'Was she—'

'She's in Bunbury Hospital. He beat her up, took her out to the car, rolled down the garage door and forgot her.'

For a while they sat in silence. Already the Australian Alps seemed like a different world.

'It doesn't make sense,' said Beverley. 'He's been out of prison for over a year. He landed a job, a decent place to live.'

'Earlier this month he failed to keep an appointment with his parole officer. He said he was sick. The parole officer got suspicious and paid him a visit at his flat.'

'And?'

'He found Levine lying on his bed, babbling about cowboys and monsters.'

Beverley picked up her orange juice and took a sip. The taste was too sweet to be healthy, but she was thirsty.

'There was something else.' Patrick noticed a woman listening and lowered his voice. 'According to the parole officer, Levine's flat was littered with letters to his sister.'

Beverley understood. 'He thinks everything can be like it was.'

'Something like that. The sixteen year old bears a striking resemblance to Claudia when she was that age.'

'You mean when she disappeared.'

'Exactly.'

'He thinks he can get Claudia back.'

'Something like that.'

'Except you think she's dead, that he killed her?'

'Yes. I'm sure of it.'

'But why? Claudia was his whole world.'

'That's what I want you to try and find out, Beverley.'

Sometimes the haze was a widening net that caught Melanie on the way down. Mostly it was a set of steel jaws that tore into her wrists and ankles. Had she only dreamed about the house and the insanity there? Then she knew. She vaguely heard the motor start up and felt the kick move through the metal hull.

She squeezed one eye open as the panel van moved up through the gears. Alone again. Was this her punishment? At least she had been spared the blindfold. Up front that heavy curtain still separated her from the other two.

The gag was tight and made her lips numb. He had reduced her world to a suitcase, a large Esky, some groceries, two large garden bags, a jerry can, a dented tool box, a shovel, a length of grubby carpet and a pillow that made her nose itch.

The curtain moved aside. The small girl was suddenly there, a picture of sadness. The pink elephant was also there. It bobbed up and down on the upholstery and then the curtain closed.

The temperature gauge red-lined and forced

Levine to coast along the flat section of highway. He needed to pull over real soon or risk cooking the motor completely. Plus the girl needed the toilet. And then the familiar P sign was suddenly there, coming up on his left. The sight of the red dirt and welcome stands of gums cheered him. He pulled in and parked well back from the bitumen roar of road trains headed up north for the big sky country. Switching off the motor, he turned in his seat and pulled back the heavy curtain.

'I have to fix the car.' It was the first time he had spoken to Melanie since Ashmere. She needed to know that what she had done at the house was bad. But Melanie did not respond. She was asleep.

'Out you get.' He'd turned to the girl. 'You can go behind a tree.'

She looked at him.

'Do you need toilet paper?'

She shook her head.

'Good. Go.'

He undid her seatbelt, leaned across her small body and opened the door for her.

The girl climbed out, walked past the front of the car and over to the thickest part of the gums.

He watched her the whole time.

Moments later she hurried back and climbed up onto her seat.

'Happy now?'

She nodded.

'Good. Do you want a drink?'

She shook her head.

'Anything to eat?'

'No.'

'Very good. That's what Monster likes to hear. Now stay in your seat.'

Releasing the bonnet catch, he stepped out of the panel van and took in some air. The girl wound down her window but made no attempt to join him. He lifted the bonnet and a fresh cloud of steam dispersed in the branches overhead. Another road train thundered past. That was some lifestyle, to be popping pills through the outback and harvesting crops of dust.

The girl toyed with the stuffed pink elephant. He smiled, bent down, picked up a good-sized rock and aimed for the open mouth of the yellow litter drum some ten metres away. Missed. He picked up another rock and missed again. He gave up on the idea, stooped a little, hopped on one foot and turned 360° through an ever-widening circle, faster and faster like the crowning moments of an Indian war dance. The girl laughed. That was new.

The approaching hire campervan caught him offguard. He walked back to the panel van and picked up the top radiator hose by the girl's feet.

'Keep smiling. Look happy.'

She squeezed the pink elephant.

'And stay in the van, okay.'

An elderly couple. He noted their South Australian licence plate. Both studied him closely as they parked in some shade of their own, twenty, thirty metres ahead. Levine disappeared behind the back of the panel van. He grabbed the tool box, slammed the rear doors shut and set to work on wrapping an old rag around the split section of hose. He spied on the couple; they seemed to be setting up camp. Two fold-up chairs had appeared and an Esky followed. The old man caught him looking and he glanced away. Too late. Smiling, the old man started to walk over.

'It's okay!' shouted Levine. 'I'm fine! Really!'

A small dog raced out from under the hire campervan and happily overtook its master's lead.

'Seen you struggling back there.' The old man stepped up to the vehicle. 'What's the problem?'

'Burst hose.' Levine kept a wary eye on the dog, which had circled the panel van twice now and was pawing at the passenger door. 'Soon be fixed though.'

'Oh, sure. Been there, done that.'

The old guy actually laughed at his own joke. His long nose wore the crusty beginnings of skin cancer.

'Say, I like your boots. Remind me of the wild west.'

Levine smiled so hard he could feel the cable of blood bulging in his neck. The hose finally pulled away in his hands and hot water splashed. The dog jumped back in surprise and barked.

'Here, Cindy. Good girl.'

Levine dropped the split hose on the ground at his feet and reached for the replacement. As he did, a loud thump came from inside the panel van. Melanie! The dog sniffed around now, moving up and down the length of the panel van. Then came a second thump, a third. The dog barked.

'Hey, what's going on?'

Levine ignored the dog's owner as he pushed the replacement hose into place. Faster, dammit. But the faster he worked, the louder the thumping got.

'Look, mister, I don't know what's going on here, but it sure don't sound right.'

Monster was suddenly there, taking shape in the clouds of steam. It drifted up into the tree branches, huge and terrible, its long snout pointed in the old man's direction.

'Look, I'm really busy.'

Levine shoved both ends together and tightened the clamps with the screwdriver.

The old man stood his ground. 'Didn't you hear what I—'

'Back off!' Levine whirled around, holding the screwdriver out in front of him.

The steam hissed, fused into an obscene shape only Levine could see. Monster curled round and over a thick limb, dropped down, down, neck stretching, muscles straining, pushing its stinking breath into the old guy's face, slowly closing the gap between them.

'Go!' roared Levine, pushing the stranger hard in the chest with his elbow.

The dog ran back to its owner, tail wagging. Quickly, the old man scooped the animal in his arms and backed away.

Melanie drew her knees up, pointed her heels and smashed down on the side of the panel van again. She thought she heard voices but couldn't be sure.

She didn't care. Someone had to hear her. Or sooner or later he was bound to make a mistake. Please, God, let it be now. She didn't intend to be another statistic for the 6.30 news.

She heard the dog. It barked and she hoped it would be enough. Up front, the girl moved the curtain aside and frowned at her.

She heard the bonnet slam down and moments later he was there, bending over the driver's seat and dropping the heavy tool box only centimetres from her face. The lid fell open and struck her above the eye. God, she was cut. She felt the blood trickle.

He started the panel van up and she kicked wildly, continuously, ignoring the pain. God, no. The panel van slid dangerously on the dirt surface as it jumped forward and picked up speed. She stopped kicking when she recognised the loud hum of bitumen beneath her body.

Had she blown it twice in one day? Then she saw the knife.

SATURDAY AFTERNOON

There were no more incidents. There had been too many already. First the house and the phone call to the police. He'd been careless to assume Melanie would do nothing. Then the old couple at the rest area, just over two and a half hours ago. That could have been the end.

Up ahead Levine saw the first of the wind-flattened trees; they seemed to crawl like holocaust survivors along the flat ground away for the sea. He wished Melanie could see them. Poor Melanie. Didn't she know he only wanted to be her friend?

The port city of Geraldton was less than thirty kilometres away, the historic Ellendale Hamlet less than five. But he had no intention of reaching either. Easing off on the accelerator, Levine saw the turn-off to the great warren of sand dunes that dominated the whole stretch of coastline. He braked, trading bitumen for dusty limestone, and drove slowly past the ruined pioneer homestead he loved to explore as a boy. The stone building fell down decades ago, long before Mumma's time even.

He drove on, first across the flat coastal plain for five kilometres, then up into the twisting chaos of the dunes. The track narrowed, at times rubbing sand into his wheels and scraping small branches against the sides of the panel van. The ride got bouncy and he hoped Melanie wasn't being bashed about too much. And steep, so steep in parts that he dropped into low gear to avoid stalling.

At the crest of the last climb he braked and the girl woke up. Her eyes widened. The Indian Ocean, vast and brooding, already in turmoil despite the lack of any sea breeze.

'We have to stay here for a while.'

She seemed too tired to understand.

'Just until I find Claudia. And until we're all rested up. Tomorrow's another long day in the saddle.'

He negotiated the steep, winding track. The motor laboured, wanted to pick up speed. In places there was no vegetation, just the sheer walls of sand on either side. Other stretches, fed by unseen springs, were wild-looking: trees, scrub, dune grasses. They followed the track through the dunes for several kilometres.

'End of the road unless you've got a four-wheel-drive.' Levine pointed to a steep circle of ridge. At its base a sheet of tin reflected the afternoon sun. 'Through there's the beach shack.'

He pulled the panel van off the track into the deepest shade.

Leo Gwyter stood waiting for them in the domestic terminal. Beverley recognised him from a newspaper cutting she had saved. Here was the new breed: tough, independent, resourceful. Up close he looked even younger.

'Welcome back to Perth.' He stepped up to Patrick, almost matching him for height, and they shook hands firmly. Next he turned to Beverley and did the same.

'I need every detail.' Their boss didn't waste any time.

Leo looked amused. His hair was long and untidy; he wore Levis and a sweatshirt.

'And you only answer to me. Understand?'

'No worries. I'll tell you all I know on the way up the coast. It's a one hour flight to Geraldton. We'll be there by 4.30 tops.'

Patrick looked puzzled.

'Information just in. A South Australian couple reported someone fitting Samuel Levine's description on the Brand Highway heading north. Got those same ol' boots his daddy left. He spooked them.'

Beverley watched the first of the luggage snake its way through the terminal.

'Everything fits. The couple pulled over at a rest area one up from Cataby Roadhouse. Levine was changing a split radiator hose.'

'And?'

'The husband heard someone in the back, banging against the side. When he asked what was going on Levine got physical, started pushing him around.'

Patrick seemed satisfied. Everything made sense so far.

'We already checked,' continued Leo. 'The mechanic at Cataby Roadhouse remembers him well. Gave the same description.'

More luggage appeared on the conveyor belt carousel.

'We'll find them. I've got every traffic cop between here and Geraldton keeping an eye out.

He won't get far.'

'How long ago did he run into the old couple?'

'Just after noon.'

'That's hours ago.' Patrick turned and waded into the crowd. 'He could be anywhere by now.'

Beverley watched him go. 'He's just tense. He's a good man.'

'Yeah, I know. Some of the old-timers filled me in.'

'Really. Then you'll know he wants a result. Badly.'

Gwyter seemed to understand. 'No worries. I'm with you, Bev.'

'It's Beverley.' She eyed him for a moment, loosened up. 'Look, I'm sorry. I guess I'm tense too.'

As they joined Patrick at the luggage pick up, a little girl in a summer dress whirled through the crowd, half-running, half-skipping. She was a splash of colour in the midst of so many grey suits. People ignored her. Not Patrick Warren. Beverley noticed the way he watched the little girl disappear into the tangle of arms, legs, briefcases. He would never relax, not while Levine was out there somewhere in fantasy land.

'Let me go!' demanded Melanie as soon as he

removed the gag. She realised they were her first words since morning. Already it seemed like a lifetime ago.

He leaned over her, his sweaty fingers running through her hair as he pulled the cloth round and loosened the knot further. She was on her side, hands tied behind her back, looking up into the face of a creep. But he was looking elsewhere.

'What's this I see?'

The knife. She had tried unsuccessfully to hide the knife in the folds of her Levis. Smiling, he picked it up and examined its sharp blade.

'Oh, but you've cut yourself.' Slowly, deliberately, he allowed the point of the blade to rest just above her eyebrow.

'Let me go.'

'You wanted to hurt me?'

'Let me—'

'You wanted to push this blade up into my chest, maybe find my heart, a lung? You disappoint me, Melanie.' He paused, turned the blade in his hands. 'I should mean much more to you than that.'

She turned her face away. All of the things he said she now wanted to do.

'Didn't your daddy ever tell you that knives are dangerous?'

He pressed the blade harder and she wanted to pull away, roll away from under its cruel point.

'Very dangerous.' He stood up, holding the knife up for her to see. In one quick, easy movement he drew the edge of the blade across his own wrist, pressing hard enough for a line of blood to erupt on his skin. 'See how sharp they can be?'

Sick. Melanie looked away. She had seen enough.

'Don't disappoint me, Melanie. I hate to be disappointed.'

'Who are you?' She turned to face him, tried to dismiss the blood freely flowing down his wrist and dripping from the tip of his index finger onto the sand.

'Oh, I'm no one special.' Finally he threw the knife back into the tool box and shut the lid. Tight. 'I'm just a good old country boy at heart.'

He leaned over her once more and she cried out.

'Shush, babe.'

'Let me go! And the girl! Now!' To hell with his disappointment. 'If you don't let us go I'll—'

'Do what, Melanie?'

His words cut sharper than any knife. She wanted to spit, to rip out his eyes.

'Please.'

He ignored her. He loosened the cord around her ankles. Without warning he bunched a fist into the waist of her Levis and roughly pulled her up to a sitting position.

'Get your hands off me!'

'Temper, temper, Melanie.' He removed his hand. 'You really should—'

'What? Be a good little girl? Play the part? Sorry. I guess I failed drama.'

He sighed loudly. 'If you'll let me finish, Melanie. You really should try and be my friend.'

'No way.'

'You need a friend. Monster can be very cruel. It would think nothing of crushing your windpipe or snapping your neck.'

Melanie said nothing. What was he saying?

'So tell me, are we friends yet?'

'If I say no will you slap me again?'

His grin returned. 'That's very good, Melanie. Very sharp.'

For the second time that day Beverley Cruz found herself looking down on the rough edge of continent.

'Brand Highway.' Leo identified the pencil-line of bitumen. 'We're right over Cataby Roadhouse.'

Patrick studied the landscape as the Cessna was

gently buffeted in small pockets of turbulence. He noted the busy roadhouse directly below.

'Mrs Webster had money.' Beverley held up a fax showing Mastercard withdrawals made in the last seventy-two hours. 'It makes him mobile.'

Her boss made no comment, but adjusted his reading glasses and returned to his own copy. She knew he was looking for leads.

'Jurien Bay is coming up on your left, folks.'

Beverley saw a small coastal community, linked by road, maybe half an hour's drive from the main highway. Within minutes they flew over the towns of Greenhead and Leeman, smaller and more isolated.

'Are those houses down there?' Beverley pointed.

'Beach shacks,' said Leo. 'They're rough as guts, not much more than a few lengths of jarrah and lots of tin sheeting. They're a big hit with the fishermen because they're hard to get to.'

Patrick looked surprised. 'You mean they're allowed to set up camp in the sand dunes?'

'Not really, but there's not much the authorities can do.'

'You don't think—' Beverley didn't get to finish her question.

'Is anyone checking it out?' Patrick eyed Leo.

'We're talking a lot of manpower.' Leo leaned forward in his seat. 'No one knows for sure how many shacks are hidden down there anyway. Dozens for sure. You'd need off-road vehicles for most of them.'

He was ignored. 'I want it checked out at first light tomorrow. A white panel van isn't going to be easy to conceal, even in that kind of environment.'

Minutes later they started the slow descent to Geraldton. Beverley saw a coastal city hemmed in by development. The whole southern end, between the sea and the highway, seemed to be a long white corridor, a rising mountain of sand. Crazily, she thought of ads for aftershave.

'That's Southgates. Enough sand down there to swallow up a small town.' Leo sucked in his breath. 'And over there on the highway is the historic Ellendale Hamlet. The small town you see behind the ridge is Ellendale itself.'

The landing was fast and bumpy. Beverley hadn't realised she was making fists until the Cessna slowed to a standstill alongside the terminal building.

It felt good to get away from the girls for a while. He'd fed them, given them a drink. He'd trusted

Melanie to take herself and the girl behind the bushes. That time the girl had needed toilet paper. He hadn't minded. Just as long as she quit crying and didn't make a mess.

No mess, Samuel. You mustn't make a mess.

So strange hearing Melanie and the girl counting slowly until they were done. A private joke. Where could they have possibly run to? He'd rewarded them with a small bar of chocolate each. That, and the possibility of an early morning swim before their Coco Pops. But only if they didn't disturb him during the night. He needed his sleep.

He'd noticed Melanie had given her chocolate bar to the girl. So sweet. Claudia would have done the same.

Now he parked the panel van at the base of the small hill. Western Australia had repeatedly rejected daylight saving, and already the sun was dropping low. Still, there was enough heat to force a sweat for a good hour or two yet. Limestone dust puffed up onto his boots as he walked to the top of the hill. Had anyone walked along this track in the last week? He doubted it. The mid-west dictated cars and air-conditioned comfort; few experienced its harsh environment by choice. No matter. Tomorrow morning they would be gone from this place, and by mid-afternoon they would be in Carnarvon with its red soil and cobalt skies.

The track levelled out and Levine abandoned it for a better view. He stepped into a dry paddock, startling some sheep that grazed there. One bolted. The rest followed. The ground was mostly barren, strewn with limestone rock and bare patches of hardened dirt. Salt crystal glistened.

He reached the highest point, sucked in his breath. There, maybe ten kilometres away, the small community of Ellendale still flourished. He even counted a few new properties, hobby farms mostly, licking the edge of the railway tracks. Passenger trains no longer snaked through the golden harvest, but Levine remembered the thunder of days long past, saw bluntly the driver's face peering down on him as he whooped and shimmied and low-circled by his mother's side. How many times had he wished it was the cowboy's face? Your daddy was no cowboy, Mumma would say. He was a monster, a bully. But Mumma had lied. She was the monster. So often she had crushed Claudia with her poison tongue.

Then he remembered where she was taking him.

No, Mumma. They'll get me worser.

He remembered her dragging him past the tall

petrol pump, the silent pub, across the narrow road that sang to an insect summer, through the gate and up the path into the primary school itself. He knew they watched her coming, those fat-faced, thin-faced boys with their wild haircuts and scuffed shoes. Whispering. Watching. But Mumma didn't care. She had Jesus in her heart and a bible by her side.

PLACES TO HIDE

The girl stood in the doorway of the beach shack with her back to Melanie. She clutched the pink elephant.

'Do you suppose he's gone for good?'

Melanie was ignored.

'Look, we need to talk.'

The girl turned to face her, then looked away again. Melanie got a shock. She looked exhausted, even sickly. God, what was he doing to her?

Melanie wished she could move her hands or feet. She was grateful for the freedom to speak, even if the freedom came with a price. Whoever he was, he was no fool. She relived the long bumpy ride and guessed they must be kilometres from the nearest help. No one would hear her cries so she saved her voice.

'Please. We have to get away from here.'

The tiny figure took a step outside and Melanie's pulse quickened.

'No. Please don't ignore me. We're in danger.'

The girl stepped back inside the beach shack. 'Monster said be good.' She spoke with great deliberation. 'Monster's in charge.'

'No, you don't understand. You must listen to me.'

'Monster will hurt Mummy. I have to be good or else.'

'But Monster isn't real.'

'Is so!'

'No, you've got to believe—'

'Is so real!' She marched up to Melanie and kicked sand. Melanie barely turned her face away in time.

'What are you doing?'

The girl stood over her, arms folded tight against her chest and that pink elephant crushed against her side. 'Is so real. I've seen Monster.'

Confused, Melanie nodded anyway. 'Okay, I believe you.'

The girl sat down directly opposite her, legs crossed. She said nothing, simply sat there, looking at her feet, toes curling in the sand.

'Do you have a name?' Melanie tried to sound calm, indifferent.

Nothing.

'My name is Melanie. I'm sixteen years old.'

'Heffalump is four.' The girl held up her pink elephant. 'Mummy gave him to me when I was born.'

'Do you know what happened to Mummy?'

Her face darkened.

Melanie changed the subject. 'Can you help me loosen my wrists? They're getting really sore.'

The request was ignored. Suddenly she was on her feet again, arms swinging by her side.

'Please.'

The girl walked back to the doorway.

A late-model Ford sedan, an unmarked pursuit vehicle, sat out in the car park. It was theirs as long as they needed it.

'Don't ask.' Leo helped carry out the luggage. 'Let's just say a friend in traffic branch owed me some.'

'This friend,' said Patrick. 'Can he get us two more like it?'

Leo hesitated. 'Sure. What the hell.'

'Good.' Patrick placed his suitcase in the boot. 'ASAP.'

The single-lane highway out from Geraldton airport fed through sheep and wheat country and onto the coastal city some fifteen kilometres away.

'What happened to the trees?' Beverley observed the gnarled trunks, bent low as if to scoop up the dust. The horizon blurred.

'Blame the wind. Weird, huh, seeing how balmy it is today. But when she's a blowin' she blows it up a treat. Reckon this place is windsurfers' paradise.'

They reached a wasteland of suburbia. Every house, every street looked familiar. It wasn't hard to imagine 20,000 separate lives clumped together here. Multiply that figure right across the state, the nation, and the thought of two girls alone with Samuel Levine was depressing.

'Why would he make a one-off payment to a Geraldton florist?' Patrick's finger moved down the Mastercard statement. He ignored the running commentary.

'Maybe he digs flowers,' joked Leo, pulling up at a set of traffic lights. 'Right there's your police station.'

Patrick pulled out his notebook and jotted something down.

'It's hot.' Beverley looked past the police station and caught a glimpse of the Indian Ocean. The water looked inviting.

'I'll get out here.' Patrick threw off his seat belt. 'There's something I want to check.'

'No, wait!' Beverley watched him. He climbed out, ignored the police station across the road and looked straight ahead.

'I'll see you both later. Arrange dinner for 6.00 sharp.'

The lights changed to green.

Levine braked hard. No, it couldn't be! He dropped into reverse and backed the panel van up a metre or so on the dusty track. There, dammit! Fresh tyre impressions, slow-curving away from the track and onto the beach.

He jumped out of his panel van and scrambled up the nearest sand dune. He didn't have to look very far. There, not more than fifty metres away, sat the ancient Land Rover. A beach rod ran the length of the vehicle.

No sign of an owner. Levine ran back to his own vehicle and drove further along the track, following the winding curves that led to the trees and the beach shack. He stopped again and ran onto the beach. This time he saw the owner, throwing a tennis ball into the breakers. The dog, a clumsy-looking golden labrador, ran playfully up to the water's edge and jumped away each time a new wave broke.

How close? One, possibly two kilometres this side of the beach shack. Did the guy even know it existed, hidden away behind the dunes? No matter. He couldn't afford the risk. He sprinted back through the heavy sand to his panel van.

Maybe he could make up a story, just long enough to get the girls away. The Land Rover was out of sight. He could say he saw two kids tampering with the fishing gear. Hell, they looked like they were stealing everything. Anything.

Foot to the floor, Levine drove at speed. He almost collected the base of a leaning tree, felt one heavy branch collide with the panel van, but he couldn't stop now. Not now, with the prize so very, very close.

The beach shack had never been intended for comfort. Melanie studied the sand floor: she saw cigarette butts, fragments of crayfish casing, numerous empty beer cans. It would be dark in an hour or two. Did he really expect them to sleep here? She didn't like to think about the loud invasion of insects on their way to join her. Or worse.

Defeated, she leaned back against the side of the beach shack in an effort to get comfortable.

Ouch!

A flap of corrugated iron curled past the jarrah support. Her forearm brushed against its sharp edge.

The girl hadn't noticed. She stood in the doorway watching the day close down.

'I wonder where we are?' Melanie tried to sound normal. She leaned slightly forward, until her fingertips located the flap of torn metal. How sharp? Sharp enough. She lined up the cord binding her wrists together. She moved her arms up and down, using all of her weight to work the cruel edge. Snagged. Jerked loose. What if she missed and ripped through an artery instead?

'Mummy's taking me to Disneyland.' Face turned away, the girl sounded happier but it was impossible to tell. 'If I'm a good girl.'

'It'll be fun.' Melanie had to keep her spirits up. 'Maybe you'll meet Minnie Mouse. Back home I have a Minnie Mouse doona.'

'What's a doona?'

Melanie never got the chance to explain. At that moment, somewhere along the beach, a vehicle slowly approached. Its heavy motor laboured in the sand.

End of the road unless you've got a four-wheel-drive.

The golden labrador padded past the doorway, its tail still visible, then steered round and poked its nose past the girl and inside the beach shack. It dropped a tennis ball at the girl's feet.

'Doggy!' The girl patted the golden labrador on the head, picked up the tennis ball and threw it outside. The animal barked.

'Over here!' shouted Melanie, as loudly as she could.

The dog fetched the tennis ball back and dropped it at the girl's feet once more. This time when she threw the ball she ran after the dog, clapping her hands wildly when it lumbered after its prize and fetched it back once more.

'Good doggy!'

The golden labrador barked loudly; Melanie noted its excited grin. Unseen, the vehicle now drew level with the beach shack.

'He-lp! We're over here!' She listened for the whine of the motor to change, to indicate that the driver was heading in off the beach and through the softer sand. 'Over here!'

With the girl outside she worked frantically on her wrists.

'Please!' The vehicle sounded so close. They had to hear. 'We need help!'

The help never came. The vehicle stayed on its original course. Melanie listened as it continued its slow journey along the beach.

'No! Don't go!'

She watched the golden labrador pick up its tennis ball for the last time and pad past the girl and the beach shack and out of sight.

'Doggy!'

The girl shouted after it but made no attempt to follow.

'Quickly! Go chase the doggy!' Melanie felt the cord jerk a notch as she pushed down hard on the protruding metal, madly sawing the frayed cord even though it sat dangerously close to her flesh. 'Go see!'

The girl just stood there, watching the dog disappear between two sand dunes and back onto the beach.

'Over here! Don't leave us!'

No use. They were already too far away. Melanie hated the fading, insect-like drone the motor made as the driver continued on.

After several minutes the cord snapped and she pulled her hands free.

'What are you doing?' demanded the girl, suddenly noticing.

Melanie ignored her and carried on working the knot binding her ankles together. There might still be a chance.

'No! That's bad!'

'It's not bad!' snapped Melanie. 'We have to get away from this place before—'

'Bad!' The girl marched up to her and her tiny fists swung wildly, sometimes connecting, mostly missing. 'Monster'll get mad!'

'Hey, quit that!'

Melanie tried to ignore the small blows raining down on her head and shoulders. Another minute passed. The knot came undone. She quickly curled her fingers through the looping cord and pulled her right foot free. Both feet.

'I said quit that!'

The girl turned and fled. Her small body dashed out of the doorway and along the rough track. Melanie jumped up and tried to give chase. At first her feet would not obey and she was forced to rest against the jarrah support to stop herself falling over. Outside, the girl stopped and watched her from a safe distance. Crazy. Couldn't she see that she was on her side, that she only wanted to help?

Something distracted the girl and she spun round. The panel van. Melanie watched it clear the last bend and brake sharply. Now it was her turn to run. She fell, picked herself up, fell again. Already he was out of the van and headed her way. Melanie cursed her swollen feet, jumped up and ran outside. Which way? Beach. If she chose the beach he wouldn't be able to drive after her. She scrambled to the top of a steep dune. Somewhere close by she heard him shouting instructions to the girl.

She saw the ocean. There was no vehicle to be seen, but she saw the disappearing curve of its tread marks, the twin impressions swallowed in places by the hissing shoreline. She charged down the soft slope, sand pulling at her legs as she went.

'Let me go!'

At the bottom of the slope his arm swung out to grab her. He must have used a shorter route. She grappled with him, pushed him off with all her might and twisted free. Running now, as fast as she could.

He was faster.

Melanie wheeled across the sand and went back the way she had come. How must it have looked to the casual observer standing along the shore? A wild game of chasey? But no one saw her desperate flight as she wheeled and turned, ducking and weaving along the beach until she found a gap between two dunes. And then *he* fell. She heard his loud, animal cry as his body pitched forward in the sand. For a moment there she thought he wasn't going to get up. When she glanced back she saw him fumbling inside his trouser pocket for something. The knife? Had she finally gotten him so pissed off that he now intended to kill her right here on the beach? No more socials. No more friends. Mum destroyed. But it wasn't the knife. Thank God it wasn't the knife.

She saw him suck on a Ventolin inhaler.

Melanie kept going. If she could just reach the panel van in time she might be able to signal for help. She ran onto the track. He couldn't be more than thirty metres behind her. Glancing back a second time she saw him getting to his feet.

Up front the girl sat in the passenger seat of the panel van. Melanie raced past her, reached the rear of the van and threw open the back doors. Tool box. She pulled the tool box over and its contents spilled out onto the grubby carpet. Matches! She tore the box apart.

'Get out!' Melanie screamed the instruction. 'Get out now!'

She dived forward, pulled the jerry can over and threw back its lid. Petrol gushed everywhere, splashing tools, soaking into the carpet.

'Get out I said!'

But the girl sat there, squeezing the pink elephant tight.

'Now!'

One look at her face said it all. She had no intention of getting out. Not now. Not ever.

'Please!'

He was suddenly there, closing the gap between them. Melanie kicked the van door. She swore loudly and dropped the matches.

CHURCH

Ocean West Hotel overlooked the calm waters of Town Beach. Just after 6.00 Patrick walked up the main staircase and into the dining room. He wore a pink carnation. The others were already seated.

'Sun's going down.' Beverley stared past the breakwater. 'The crayfishing boats will be heading in to beat the dark.'

Patrick merely glanced at the views. Maybe under different circumstances he would have found the seascape interesting. He joined them at the table.

'It's been a long day,' observed Beverley. 'I'm bombed.'

Patrick slipped on his reading glasses and scanned the menu. 'It's going to be an even longer night.'

'He might run,' said Leo. 'Try to slip through under the cover of darkness.'

Patrick shook his head. 'He doesn't know we're here, remember? And anyway, this is where he grew up.'

'Where Claudia grew up,' added Beverley. She eyed a large oil tanker several kilometres out to sea. 'He won't leave until he's got what he came for.'

'His sister, right?' Leo shook his head. 'I can't believe he'd come all this way just to dig up a pile of bones.'

A waitress arrived. All discussion ceased until she took their drinks order.

Patrick cut some slack. 'Eat well. Tonight I want you to coordinate local police efforts.'

Leo nodded.

'Make sure they're ready to check every beach shack north and south of here. Cover every track.'

Again, Leo nodded. Satisfied, Patrick turned to Beverley.

She already knew what to do: stay by the fax, all night if necessary. Melbourne had promised an update on Levine's childhood.

'What about you, Patrick?' She sipped her drink. 'The usual?'

'I'm off to church.'

Beverley and Leo both looked at him.

'Just routine. He sent some flowers to an old church out of town. If it's the church I think it is—'

At that moment a uniformed officer walked into the dining room and scanned the tables. Patrick waved him over. The officer carried a message, which Patrick paraphrased for the others. The news was disturbing. Marion Webster had signed a statement which alleged Samuel Levine had paraded her in front of her daughter on the day he took over their home.

'And?'

'Apparently he wore a gruesome rubber mask at the time. Called himself Monster. He demonstrated what Monster was capable of if little Christine didn't do exactly as she was told.'

'That's sick,' said Leo.

Beverley tried thinking of something else. Outside, across the bay, a lone windsurfer gave up on the balmy conditions.

He meant to finish the game forever. Melanie wished the gag and blindfold could fade away, the new cord simply dissolve into vapour on her wrists. He hadn't bothered with her ankles. Lying in the rear of the panel van, on her side, she wondered if she wasn't dead already. Hadn't he taken her from her home two nights ago, made her life his own and turned her—invisible?

Petrol fumes clawed at her mouth, her nostrils and eyes. She felt dizzy, sick. Escape or die: all the choices in her life had been reduced to that simple truth. And with the blindfold in place wasn't she already tasting the darkness? So what flavour was death?

A bumpy ride. Melanie figured he was still driving down the track parallel with the beach. Some joke. She hadn't even seen the beach, except for a glimpse when she fled the beach shack. She thought she heard a distant thunder of breaking waves. Or was it just the petrol fumes mixing up the craziness of her ordeal? She no longer knew anything. Brad always said she knew nothing and maybe he was right. It bugged her the way boys were always right. Wouldn't he get a surprise when he saw the headlines!

A sudden bump threw her hard against the side of the panel van. The track climbed a steep incline and cleared the other side. More climbs followed before the ride eventually flattened out. She figured they were now heading away from the sea.

After a minute or so the van slowed almost to a stop and the track disappeared completely as they took a sharp left.

Bitumen: smooth, loud, fast. Melanie tried to work out how fast. Country fast. Not for long, though. Again the van slowed, took a sharp right that rolled her onto her stomach. Almost immediately she noticed the climb, long and steep, much steeper than anything so far. They seemed to fly down the other side.

After a few more minutes the van slowed down, braked, stopped. She recognised the click-click-click of the indicator. He turned left, braked again and the van's tyres slapped railway tracks. Several kilometres on, the bitumen roar once again gave way to an unsealed surface. Where the hell was he taking them?

Ten minutes later she got her answer.

'Been a while,' he said, talking to himself. Wasn't that the first sign of madness? Some joke. Whoever he was, he was cracked in the head, writer and director of his very own road movie.

He parked the panel van, opened up the rear doors and dug deep inside the tool box for something. Melanie heard the dull clatter. God, if she could only be Supergirl and pull her cord apart like tissue paper. Or be like Christopher Pike and figure out some ridiculous solution to her problem.

'Right. Let's go.'

He led her across some open ground. At the year eleven camp being blindfolded had been fun. Trust games taught you to care for one another, even if Rachel had accidentally on purpose walked her into Mr Reynolds. So embarrassing when her hand brushed against his crotch. This was different, scary. The ground felt hard and barren. Where was she? Where was he leading her? There was no sound she recognised. No traffic noises. Nothing at all. He stopped.

'Don't move.'

She heard him take two more steps forward and tried to work out the sound. Like that time when she was small and she watched her father prise apart that old wooden pallet he had salvaged from the Ashmere tip. That was the happiest summer. Dad built her the best cubby in the street. But first he had to prise the planks of wood apart and—

Door! He was prising a door open. There was a loud *crack* and she heard his corny cowboy boot kicking it in. The next sound confirmed her guess. Creaking hinges sounded the same wherever you went.

She felt his rough hand upon her shoulder. Where was the girl? Probably back at the panel van squeezing Heffalump for all she was worth. He dragged her inside some place where the air was clean and cool.

'I want to show you something.'

He pulled her blindfold down, but not her gag, and she saw they were standing in the middle of an old empty church. The building had been stripped bare.

'Is this the first time you've been inside one?'

She deliberately ignored his question. Sure, he could tie her up, push her around, but he couldn't make her nod and shake her head like some circus trick pony.

Or could he?

He didn't press the matter, simply sighed and steered her across a bare wooden floor, dusty with the years, to the nearest window. The window looked south.

'Look. This is where Claudia plays.'

Wheat fields. Their golden harvest swayed and stretched into infinity. And sky. The sky was turning the colour of blood. She almost tripped as he rushed her across to the opposite wall. The view was almost identical: more wheat fields. The only landmark was a derelict farm shed a full kilometre away, almost leaning over the unsealed road. Directly in front of her, less than twenty metres away, she saw the panel van. Yep, there sat the girl with Heffalump.

'And here.' He spun her around. Was that the flash of a headstone she saw? 'And here.' More wheat as he dragged her across the floorboards. His voice echoed in the large empty building. 'She's around here somewhere.'

His fingers gripped her shoulder, hard, and he marched her to the altar at the far end of the church, directly opposite the main door they had just entered. She struggled, even mumbled her protests into the gag. He merely laughed as he pulled her up onto the platform and threw open the small concealed trapdoor. Three solid jarrah steps hovered above the dark place. Could he really mean to go through with this?

'Monster hates bad children. You should have been good when you had the chance.' Again his rough hands spun her around as he stepped her up to the edge. 'You'll just have to stay here while I go and find Claudia.'

No way!

She kicked out and her heel caught him on the

shin. He got mad. In one swift movement he was pushing her by the hair and shoulders and bundling her down the steps and into the shallow darkness below.

Never!

The trapdoor echoed loudly inside the empty building. She heard him wedge something into place.

Let me—

But he was going already. Melanie heard those same hinges creak as he slammed the heavy door behind him. Seconds later she heard the panel van fire up and pull away. Great. Now what? Monster hates bad children? Well, screw Monster. She should have gone with Brad after all. Surfing wasn't that bad. Now she was stuck in some dark corner of hell—hungry , thirsty, totally pissed.

Hey, don't lose it. Stay on top.

She breathed in, counted one, two, three, four, breathed out. Whenever she did that with Brad he laughed at her. Well, screw Brad, too.

She quickly discovered that it was not entirely dark. Even though the trapdoor above her head sat flush with the rest of the stage area, a middle hinge was missing and the wood had warped. She noticed the gap and pressed her face against the rapidly fading light. It offered her only view of the outside world. Not much of a world anymore, just a sad empty church. Its thick walls of pioneer stone and solid roof of exposed jarrah had failed to keep the faithful. No preacher rolled out his message of God and salvation. No congregation jumped to its feet and answered the call to arms.

He had driven off and left her here. Melanie remembered his question. Had she ever been inside a church before? Yes, once, in the city two years ago. She had been curious, fifteen minutes away from a movie and all alone. The church was large and cool, mostly empty. Did God really live there? She couldn't see how. The place was musty. Walking up the front, past the worn pews and brass ornaments, she saw the altar and moved towards it. At the same moment she saw the priest, old, tired-looking. He was about to say something, but she turned and left in a hurry. Outside the sun was hot and made her blink. Traffic chaos chased her back into lunchtime crowds. That was church: musty smells and old men fused into one.

They probably used this place beneath the stage for baptisms. Melanie pictured herself dressed in a white flowing robe, kneeling in the water while a preacher spoke prayers and scripture verses over her. She imagined the smiling congregation, old folk fanning themselves in the heat. Gently the preacher leaned her back into the water until she was fully immersed.

Only, it wasn't a preacher at all. The hands moved up to her throat and squeezed down into her windpipe. She tried to scream and her lungs frothed up into a meeting of water and garbled sound. The old folk jumped to their feet and urged him on. Brad, too, standing alone in the back row. And her father from a year ago.

No, not real!

Melanie shook off the image and sat up straight. She was sweating now and her heartbeat raced. Why did she have to turn everything into a video clip? She gulped air from the darkness.

REUNION

He had been wise to hide the panel van behind the falling shed. He'd left the girl asleep and now he was glad of his decision.

Levine ducked, watched the late-model Falcon float past in a cloud of dust and metal. A cop for sure. He pulled into a crouch position in the tall wheat and watched the brake lights, then the reverse lights, as the vehicle backed up to draw level with the deserted church. Someone got out.

He moved forward, keeping his eye on the cop. No ordinary cop, however. The clean lines of the suit and that ridiculous carnation suggested a man with an eye for detail. Observant, too, as he studied the old stone building carefully and approached on foot. No matter. He would be dealt with.

Levine flattened himself against the end wall. He heard the footsteps coming around the side of the church. He looked at the quiet gravestones, the golden storm beyond. Now was the time for Monster to show its strength.

The footsteps suddenly stopped.

Melbourne didn't waste any time. Back at Geraldton police station the fax arrived just after 7.00. Beverley snatched up the page and digested the update.

'Claudia didn't just run away.' She looked up at the wall map. 'Small town. Small town gossip. Why didn't I think of it sooner?'

'You got something, Ms Cruz?' The young constable stopped typing.

'There's still a primary school in Ellendale, right?'

'Sure is.' Stretching his legs Constable Ross Peters stood up from his mound of paperwork and walked over. 'Matter of fact they're putting on a big show next week.'

'What kind of show?'

'Oh, you know. Old school reunion. Class of whatever.'

She read the page more carefully. 'It must have

been hard on young Samuel. No father. Harsh mother. Lots of teasing. And just when things were looking up, Claudia turned sixteen and took off.'

'Ms Cruz?'

'Get Patrick on his car radio. Tell him I'll join him at the church.'

The constable looked puzzled.

'Just say I got some fresh information and I'm on my way.' She headed for the door. 'Where's Leo?'

'He isn't back from the hotel yet.'

'Well, get him. Tell him to stay on the police channel. We may need him.'

The constable shook his head. 'But what's any of this got to do with the missing girls?'

'Maybe everything.' Beverley folded up the fax and pushed it deep inside her pocket. 'Just before she quit school, Claudia told one of her teachers she thought she was pregnant. My guess is she was raped. That's why she disappeared, to escape her mother's wrath and the boys responsible. I think it also explains why Levine is back.'

'To come looking for her?'

'For revenge.'

'You don't think he killed her?'

'As far as I can tell Samuel Levine loved his sister.'

'You mean like he loved his mother?'

Beverley said nothing.

Melanie thought she heard the panel van pull up just moments ago, but now she wasn't so sure. She strained to listen. Moments later a face appeared at the nearest window and she saw at once that it wasn't him. Who then? It didn't matter; the stranger gave her hope. No, something greater than hope.

She thought quickly. With so much of her movement in her arms and legs restricted, her only chance lay in using the rest of her body. She leaned over onto her side and a fresh explosion of pain found her. She had forgotten the wooden steps; her head fell forward with a sickening thump and she collapsed onto her back. Gasping for air, she tried to ignore the pain and concentrated on the trapdoor directly above her face. Even if it wouldn't budge, she would make it sing.

She kicked. She had no idea if the stranger was even still there, but she kicked anyway. Kicked. Smashed the square of wood with all of her weight.

Inside the baptismal pool the sound cannoned. She hoped it would echo up through the whole building and through to the outside. He had to hear! What other chance did she have?

Patrick Warren stepped back from the window and walked round the side of the church. He wanted to check out the grave for himself.

The small plot behind the church contained a handful of graves. Only one retained a sun-scorched bouquet. Patrick walked over, momentarily distracted by the sea of ripe wheat that seemed to stretch forever. Someone had been through there recently. He saw the way the tall crop had been pushed back in places.

Later. First he turned his attention to the headstone. It was hard to read the inscription. Time and season had chipped away at the limestone slab. He kneeled down for a better look. He could just make out all four names: Frederick Levine, beloved husband to Mary, devoted father to Samuel and Claudia. Some joke. There had been little love in that relationship. A shearer who lived for the open road, Frederick Levine had died in a pub brawl the same month Claudia was born. Young Samuel was only three years old. All his father had left him was a pair of fancy cowboy boots for his tiny feet to grow into. Mary Levine turned to religion and, according to some, went a little crazy along the way. Most of that craziness had slow-trickled into her son.

'Hi, there!'

The tall shadow cut across his path and he jumped to his feet, startled.

Levine's voice was sing-song. 'Come to listen to the cowboy, huh?'

Patrick ducked a moment too late. He groaned in anticipation as the shovel cut a wide arc through the air.

At last! Melanie listened to the sounds of freedom. First she heard the low, creaking yawn of the church door. Next she heard the sound of footsteps on the ancient jarrah floorboards. There was a pause and she seized her chance.

Her world boomed; he had to hear. She kicked again and again, so hard and fast that she thought the trapdoor might very well crack in two.

She stopped. Why wasn't he coming over? Awkwardly she pulled herself up into a sitting position once more and shuffled across the floor. She pressed her eye to the gap.

Him! She recognised his cowboy boots. He had his back to her and was dragging something over.

He stepped out of her line of vision, only to return seconds later, one large round eye staring at her in the dark and the kind of voice that sent small children running to their parents' room.

'Miss me?'

She lost it then, jerking her head back against the wall, pulling so hard on the cord binding her wrists that her pulse seemed to fire warning shots.

The trapdoor swung open. He leaned over her. Both his arms were caked in dirt and she tried desperately to see what it was he had dragged across the floor.

'I baptise thee in the name of Frankenstein, Dracula and the Wolfman.' His laughter was loud and he pulled her onto her feet and up the steps. 'Claudia's waiting in the van. Tonight we set off for the promised land.'

That crazed look from this morning rose up to haunt her.

'Close your eyes, Melanie.'

She immediately did as she was told. Was this where he would finish his hideous game? She felt his eyes burning through her clothes, past flesh and bone, deep into her soul.

'Good. Now keep those eyes shut tight.'

Was he about to leap upon her again, to clamp that suffocating rag against her mouth and nose like last time? She listened hard and thought she heard the rustle of a paper bag.

'Turn round slowly, Melanie.'

She turned, slowly, eyes shut tight.

'Stop!'

She stopped. Now she had her back to him. The paper rustled some more and she knew it could only be a matter of time. She fought to stay in control.

His hands touched the back of her neck and she swallowed hard. He removed the gag.

'What have you done to the girl?'

He ignored the question. 'Turn around, Melanie.'

His voice! It wasn't the same.

'No! Please!'

'I said turn around, Melanie.'

His voice had changed, grown deeper. Muffled, too, as if she was hearing him through fog.

'Now, Melanie.' He spun her round to face him, to face whatever it was he wanted her to see.

She opened her eyes.

'Like it?'

He wore a rubber mask, one of those ghoulish creations found in any joke shop across the land. He quickly tore it off and stood there grinning like a smart-arsed little boy.

'I asked if you liked it?' Only, he didn't mean the

mask. His thumb pointed over his shoulder, to a bloodied mess on the church floor.

'Let me go!' snapped Melanie, not caring anymore. She had passed that point. 'And the girl! We're not animals! You can't own us!'

For a moment he looked at her, puzzled. She caught the look.

'Now! Let us go!'

'I can't.' He grew serious once more. 'We're family.'

Evening became night. Western Australia turned down the heat. Beverley Cruz turned down the air-conditioner. The pioneer church was exactly where the young constable said it would be. She saw Patrick's vehicle parked alongside the building, slowed to a crawl and pulled over. Patrick's passenger-side door was thrown open.

Now she was scared. Beverley switched off the ignition and called in her location.

'Do you need back-up?' crackled a now-familiar voice from Geraldton CIB.

'I'm not sure.' She looked for another vehicle, any sign of danger. 'Is Leo there yet?'

'Been and gone.'

After sundown the wheat fields looked eerie,

alive. She found herself dismissing the thought of ghosts.

'Ms Cruz?'

'I'm still here.' She told him to expect an okay in ten minutes, got out of the car and breathed the evening into her system. The church looked peaceful enough. So why had Patrick left the car door wide open? Instinctively her hand moved up to her shoulder holster and she undid the clip. She proceeded with caution, her shoes scuffing the dusty limestone track. When she drew level with the vehicle she immediately understood. Patrick's radio: every wire had been ripped out and strewn on the front passenger seat.

Beverley took out her handgun. She sprinted from the car to the side of the church and peered in through a window. No movement inside. Was anyone hiding behind the heavy door? She rounded the corner of the building and paused at the stone doorstep. Blood!

'Police! Stand back!'

Nothing. She kicked the door open, fell back against the stonework. Still nothing. Gun raised, she ducked inside, glanced left, right, and immediately behind the door itself. The blood led to a small altar up the far end. She saw an open trapdoor.

'Patrick?'

No reply. Beverley proceeded across the wooden floor, avoiding the blood, gun drawn level, eyes darting from window to window and back to the trapdoor.

'This is the police. If you can hear me, indicate now.'

Still no reply. She stepped up onto the platform and flattened herself against the back wall, handgun out in front of her.

'Last chance.'

Beverley peered into the baptismal pool. Which worked first, eyes or nose? There just below, in a twisted parody of nature, lay the remains of a large dog. Beverley saw the matted golden hair, the translucent bones sticking through the torn flesh. She was already taking a half-step back when she noticed movement outside the doorway.

She whirled around, her training sending her into a crouch position.

Patrick Warren fell forward through the open doorway, his head striking the jarrah frame as he went down.

PAY BACK

How those little bitches loved to laugh while the boys beat him up.

Dobber! Gonna get ya after school! Gonna punch ya lights out!

Shoved. Pushed. All part of the schoolyard blues.

'Let's see them try tonight. We'll show them!'

Ellendale after dark was a grid of silence stretching nowhere. Only the pub showed any sign of life: he saw the half-empty jug of beer standing on the windowsill while its owner lined up a shot with a pool cue. Mumma had always said they killed the cowboy in a pub just like it. Sometimes she'd smiled as she said it.

The general store was shut. The railway museum

was shut. Up ahead he saw the garage with its solitary Ampol pump. Shut. A car wreck sat on blocks behind cyclone gates.

No, nothing had changed. Ellendale's slow poison trickled back into his veins, squeezed open his eyes and made him remember every blow, every bruise, every schoolyard taunt. The railway crossing was a slap in the face. He blinked. Ellendale Primary School floated into view and he slowed down, braked, pulled off to the side of the road.

'Stay in the car.' He turned to the girl, now wide awake, and saw she clutched her pink elephant tighter than ever. She refused to look at him. No matter. Once his business was finished here they would go somewhere nice.

He switched off the motor and killed the headlights. The school hadn't changed much: same old architecture, with its single high-pitched roof and long wooden verandah. Practical. On hot days the tall building cast a huge net of shade over the bitumen lake.

He remembered how it had been. By the time Mumma reached the school gates everyone had marched single file into the classrooms. That day was hot, ready to explode.

No, Mumma. Please.

Walk tall, Samuel. We have the Lord Jesus on our side.

But Mumma—

She dragged him along the wide bitumen path and past the slow chig-chig-chig of a lawn sprinkler. Deep inside the school the insect chorus buzzed and drilled: chairs scraping, kids yelling, a teacher's voice calling the roll. A small kid appeared on the verandah and went to his bag. He fished out his wooden pencil box and hurried back inside.

Mumma shook her head and looked past him to the railway crossing, the distant wheat bins, Ellendale's one lonely main street. He wished she would listen.

Mumma never listened.

Now the same school lay in darkness as he climbed out of the panel van and walked round to the rear. Melanie would see this. She would see him pour petrol on the school, light a match, know he meant business. He would do it for the cowboy. And Claudia.

'Know what I'm saying! Never let the bullies think they've won!'

He threw open the rear doors. 'What the—'

Melanie's legs and feet scrambled through the curtain and he heard her fumbling with the driver's door. He noted the open lid of the tool box, saw the broken hacksaw blade lying next to her torn cord. Clever. Very clever.

'Melanie! Don't make me cross now!'

In one quick movement he rounded the side of the panel van and sprinted after her.

'So you want to play primary school games, huh? Kiss chasey? Tag? Sure, we can play games!'

Beverley Cruz stayed by the radio. She wanted to be sure.

'They should be almost there by now.' The voice crackled on the radio. Somewhere out back other voices sounded loud, excited.

'Okay, get me some local knowledge down here. What about the constable?'

'The young bloke? Sure. Why not? He's been itching to leave his desk all evening.'

Beverley sucked in her breath. 'Tell him to make it fast.'

'Gotcha.'

'And another thing. It's too dark to be effective. Get a police chopper here ASAP. I don't care what it takes.'

The call ended and she eyed the sky. A large, round moon broke the skin of the ridge.

Patrick didn't look good. He was slumped over in the doorway.

'Patrick, can you hear me?'

'Wheat field.' He tried pointing over his shoulder, past the small graveyard, and grimaced in pain. 'Make them—search.'

'Patrick, please. You've got to—'

'Claudia.' He coughed hard and a thin line of blood trickled from the corner of his mouth.

Beverley knelt down beside him and undid the top two buttons of his shirt. His breathing stopped.

'Patrick!'

Quickly, she pulled him down onto the floor, tilted his head back and pinched his nostrils. Sirens wailed in the darkness, grew louder as she lifted his jaw forward with her free hand, took a deep breath and placed her mouth firmly over his. Breathe one second, two seconds, release. She turned her head sideways and saw his chest falling. Again. Breathe, one second, two seconds, release.

All around her the evening exploded with noise, lights, movement. She heard car doors slam.

Running feet.

'We'll take over, Miss!'

Breathe, one second, two—

Patrick coughed abruptly, violently as some unseen hand pulled her to one side.

'Beverley?'

She turned round, numb, dysfunctional.

'He'll be fine. The ambulance is here.'

Leo Gwyter stepped up to her, placed his arm around her waist and steered her out of the way. More police cars arrived. She watched Patrick being loaded onto a stretcher while someone played a spotlight over the church and immediate surroundings.

Melanie ran into the school. She took the steps two at a time and her feet pounded on the long wooden verandah. If she could outrun him and hide until daybreak she might survive his madness.

A solitary security light allowed her to see the way dimly as she glanced back over her shoulder. He had stopped, was bent over and clutching his knees, eyes fixed on her. Then she saw the gun.

Crack!

The bullet punched a fingerhole in the zincalume sheeting above her head. Melanie crouched down into shadow. Across the railway tracks a dog ignited in the fury. Other dogs.

Crack!

She jumped. Somewhere behind her the bullet slammed into wood. Shouts spilled out of the darkness from the direction of the pub.

'Don't make me hurt you, Melanie. We're family, remember?'

The girl stepped up onto the verandah and walked over. Melanie yelled out but she wasn't fast enough.

'See? Family.'

The girl walked over to him, sobbing loudly. After everything he had subjected her to, how could she go anywhere near him? Then Melanie remembered. Monster. As real to her impressionable mind as anything in the physical world.

'Leave her be, you big bully!'

'Sure. Anything you say, Melanie.' He lifted both arms in the air. 'Look, Ma! No hands!'

The girl made no attempt to move away. Worse, she moved closer. Levine laughed. In the same moment he gently gathered her to him.

'She's just a little kid!'

Dogs barking. Men shouting.

'Oh, she's much more than that.' Levine stroked

her hair gently and whispered something in her ear.

'Okay. You win.' Melanie stepped back into the dim light. She couldn't hide. Levine had contaminated all that he had touched in his own world; now he wanted to contaminate the girl's world. No more Minnie Mouse. Forget Disneyland. Everything would be black and bruising, corrupt beyond repair.

'That's right, Melanie.' He watched her closely. 'Come to Daddy.'

Without warning he spun round and took the three men approaching from the pub by surprise. He fired one shot above their heads. The men dived for cover, scrambling and cursing. Melanie watched them crawl along the ground and flatten themselves against the trunk of a large white gum.

'Good decision, men!' He eyed her now, waving the gun towards the panel van. 'Let's go, Melanie.'

He was already rushing the girl back down the steps and across the lawn. He lifted her up and pushed her inside the rear of the van. He produced the jerry can, walked back to the verandah and pulled the lid. He splashed petrol everywhere, the jerry can against his side, spilling a long line behind him. He continued down the verandah towards her.

Melanie couldn't breath properly. He couldn't be serious.

'Please get back in the van, Melanie.' He stopped pouring the petrol. 'Unless you want to join Mumma.'

A second set of steps led off the verandah. She did as she was told. As soon as she climbed into the back of the panel van he started to follow her, hesitated. She saw him walk over to a classroom, press the barrel of the gun against the door lock and squeeze the trigger.

'Cooee!'

The lock shattered. He kicked open the classroom door and splashed petrol over the carpet. Gun in one hand, half-empty jerry can in the other, he backed out of the classroom and along the verandah, walked over to the panel van, threw the container in the back and slammed the rear doors shut.

'No, not that!' From her safe place Melanie followed his progress back to the school verandah. He carried a box of matches.

'Better run, men! Run or die!'

The three men understood at once, jumped to their feet and took their chances.

Crack!

The bullet slammed home. Horribly, one man's hand dropped to his knee to try and push everything back in place. But his weight, and the shock to the system, brought him down hard on the school lawn and Melanie couldn't look away. Videos lied. This wasn't exciting. This was sad. She watched anyway, felt dirty in the process.

'No!' screamed Melanie. 'Wait. I'll do anything you ask.'

'Promise?'

'Yes!'

'You're lying.'

'Truth! Cross my heart.'

'Tell me about your father, Melanie. Did he touch you?'

'No. Oh, God.'

'But he tried, right?'

She said nothing. He shook the matchbox.

'Right, Melanie?'

'He tried to. Last year when Mum wasn't in.'

'But you wouldn't let him right? Truth now.'

'I fought him.'

'How?'

'I—' Buried hostility boiled up inside of her. 'I kicked him. I scratched his face.'

'You wanted to hurt him, Melanie? You wanted to

get even for all those times he'd stared at you from across the room? Am I right?'

'No. It wasn't a case of—'

'Mum had always pretended it wasn't happening and you wanted some pay back for all the times he touched you. It's true, isn't it?'

'No! No, he never touched me. I already told you. He—'

'Nice try, Melanie.' Smiling, he took out a match and struck it. The small flame flared up, immediately started to burn down. 'Time to go nigh-nighs!'

He dropped the match, turned and ran, whirling the gun around his head and—*crack*—fired one last round at the wild night.

Whumph!

The sprinting wall of flames seemed to suck the night away. Here was hellfire and plenty of it. Melanie tore her gaze away, only to see the rising inferno mirrored in the girl's tear-filled eyes.

He didn't care. He strolled over, calmly fell behind the wheel and glanced back over his shoulder to where she and the girl sat huddled together.

'I guess we showed 'em, huh?'

He drove slowly away. Melanie noticed he didn't

once look back at the fiery landscape. She felt dirty. Violated. How could he have known?

Constable Ross Peters arrived at the church just as the news came through. Levine had Patrick's gun. Someone was shot. The school was burning down.

'Ms Cruz—'

'Sshhh!' Beverley listened hard. The chopper would take one hour, maybe two. When the message was over she threw down the handset and stepped back from the police car. 'I don't believe this.'

Leo rushed over. 'You hear?' He thumbed over his shoulder in the direction of Ellendale. A red glow smudged the horizon. 'Bastard's got balls.'

Beverley moved round the front of the car. 'Ross, you're driving.'

'But—'

'Ellendale Primary School.' She threw him the car keys. 'We'll explain on the way.'

'Right.'

'And drive fast, Ross.'

Up front two patrol cars quickly pulled away, their blue lights raking the wheat fields on either side. Constable Ross Peters turned the key in the ignition, flicked on the headlights, the blue lights, and pushed his foot flat to the floor. He spun the wheels, quickly accelerated through the gears. Leo fell into the back seat, breathing hard.

'Where does Ellendale Road lead to?' asked Beverley.

'Back across the ridge. Down past the historic hamlet and through to the North West Coastal Highway.' Leo laughed. 'Turn left for Perth. Turn right for Darwin. Either way he's stuffed. We've got road blocks set up in Dongara and Northampton.'

'Unless he heads for the beach.' Ross overtook the two patrol cars up front and welcomed the open road. 'Don't forget there's a turn-off about a kilometre along the highway.'

'And?'

'Takes you through to the sand dunes.'

'Southgates, right?' Beverely remembered Leo pointing them out earlier that day as they came in to land. 'Take me there.'

'No way!' Leo swore. 'That's the last place he'd be headed!'

'Do it, Ross. It's our best chance of finding him tonight.' She snatched up the handset and informed Geraldton police station. 'And let me know the moment that chopper arrives, understand?'

They understood.

The constable took a sharp left, passed houses, a pub, the railway museum and garage. A handful of locals stood in front of the general store. An ambulance screamed past as they bounced across the railway crossing. They slowed down for the old school.

'Don't stop, Ross.'

A traffic patrolman allowed them to squeeze through the litter of emergency vehicles. Beverley watched the volunteer fire brigade tackling the tall flames as they passed. No way. Not with that old equipment. Most of the locals stood helplessly by.

'That was my old school,' said Ross softly, almost crawling through the heap. 'It's like someone just ripped up my childhood.'

Two small girls stood side-by-side on the opposite pavement, their mothers desperately trying to comfort them. Overhead, the full moon cast a ghostly sheen over the wheat fields.

MONSTER

For a long time he said nothing. He walked the girls across the sand and made them sit in the doorway of the shack while he leaned against the panel van. Melanie looked tired. She had to realise who was in charge. No blindfold or gag this time. No tying up. He thumbed the barrel of the gun and stared at her. She stared back at him. No matter. She would learn, the hard way.

At least the girl had stopped her silly nonsense. She had no right to cry like that. In the weeks to come, away from her doting mother—

Mumma?

—the girl would learn not to be such a sook.

A familiar song came on the radio and he was jolted by the memory of blood on his hands. Not his doing, but Monster's. And soon Monster would be back for more. He sensed its misshapen features grinning back at him from the lifeless moon. He tossed the gun onto the driver's seat.

Monster jumped back to earth.

'Leave me alone, Mumma!'

A looping shadow, now there, now gone, he heard the slap of beating wings in his hair as he kicked sand, spun round and round, willing Monster to go away.

'I don't need you any more!'

Monster stayed. It carved tunnels through the warm night air, claws outstretched, jaw snapping. It pushed its stinking snout into his face and roared so loud that he clutched his head in both hands. He dropped down onto his knees and watched helplessly as Monster floated across the sand to where the girls sat in silence.

'But they're mine, Mumma! You promised!'

Monster billowed up behind Melanie and the girl, filling the doorway, huge and terrible. Its lips parted and he heard its menacing hiss.

'No, you can't have them! They're family!'

Both girls watched him. Neither girl saw Monster towering over her head, its own head looping down, down, lips and teeth a crackling dance.

'Mine!'

Monster tossed back its head, roared, jumped into the sky, ten, twenty metres above the beach shack, beyond the tallest tree, higher than the steepest slope of sand. It hovered, seemed to melt into the night sky and was gone.

Levine breathed deeply. He struggled to his feet. Monster's visit had left him with a migraine the size of a steam shovel slamming around inside his skull.

Melanie sat in the doorway, not daring to move. She studied him with such intensity.

'Stop staring!'

He should switch off the radio, kill the headlights before the battery went flat. No matter. First he needed music, some light, a place to dance. He stood tall again and his shadow raced across the sand to stop Melanie staring. He needed to relax. Ignore Monster and it would stay away. He started to move. Faster. Faster. His tall man's shadow dipped and curled on the side of the beach shack. But the moon spun round and round, matching him step for step, and Monster's grin widened. Mumma's grin!

'Stay away, dammit! You're dead. I heard your screams.'

He ran to the panel van and turned up the volume. When he walked back into the dull light Claudia was suddenly there, growing out of the shadows on tin. She floated towards him, her fingers of ash and bone outstretched before her, that party dress he loved so much billowing behind.

'Claudia! Tell Mumma to stay away.'

She draped her cold hands around his neck and he slowly stopped turning. As he did, her body settled weightlessly into his arms like a falling leaf to soil. Her fingers moved up from his neck and into his hair and he studied her face, smooth as washed stone. She slowed down the pictures as he carried her over to meet the others.

'See. Didn't I say we were family?'

Melanie was about to say something, but a slow song started to play and moved him back into the light. He danced a waltz.

'Come join us.'

Neither girl moved.

'Now!'

Slowly, Melanie helped the girl to her feet and they walked over.

'Now dance.'

Melanie took the girl's hands in her own and

they started to move to the music. Across the dunes he could hear the DJ of the sea playing out his own play-list. Perfect.

The song on the radio ended. He danced anyway. It was only when he looked up that he sensed their confusion.

'There is no Claudia.' Melanie stared at him like he was insane. 'There's just us.'

Even before the statement was completed Levine felt Claudia sinking down through his hands, his arms. He tried to hold onto her, desperately clutched her body of mist. He watched her pale face looking up at him as she slowly sank into the ground, grains of sand trickling into her ears and mouth, up her nose and into her eyes. Did she say something just before she slipped beneath the ground?

He shut out the image. When he looked again he saw the face of Monster, grinning up at him from the sand.

'Go away!'

He rushed back to the passenger-side window, picked up the gun, aimed and squeezed the trigger. The bullet shattered the AM/FM radio. An old Ry Cooder song sparked and was gone.

But not Monster.

Kill, them, brother! Just like you killed me!

'Shut up!' Levine smashed the butt of the gun hard against his forehead, once, twice, again and again until Monster's voice splintered into a thousand pieces. A thousand voices cried back in unison.

'I said—'

Shut up shut up shut up shut up! taunted Monster, louder, meaner, the biggest bully of them all.

Levine walked over, pointed the gun and fired into the sand. Monster shrieked and the fireball of its melting face swung up into his own. It hovered there and the nerve endings under his skin began to tingle and twitch.

'Away!'

He squeezed off one more shot. The bullet demolished Monster's features and it was gone. Vanished. No more. He lifted his eyes to the night sky and in his ears he heard the sound of creeping things. He saw blood on the moon.

Melanie watched it all. Levine tossed his head back, as if shaking off water. He spiralled, once, twice, digging the heels of his boots into the sand to save his balance.

'Let's go,' she whispered to the girl. 'No arguments.'

For once the girl didn't argue. Maybe she finally realised who Monster was. Or maybe she was in shock.

'Hold my hand tight.'

As soon as she felt the small hand in her own, Melanie ran. The girl ran beside her, as fast as her little legs would allow.

'Stop! Now!'

Melanie glanced back. He finally noticed them, jumped forward, stumbling in the sand, and gave chase.

'No way!' she yelled. 'We're leaving!'

'I'll shoot.'

The girl started to cry; Melanie hauled her across the sand.

'Stop I said!'

'Go ahead. Shoot.'

Behind her she heard his animal cry. Up ahead she saw a wall of sand looming above them in the dark.

'I mean it, Melanie. I'm not kidding.'

'Mister, you haven't got the balls.'

Crack.

The girl cried out, went crashing down and Melanie almost tripped over her small body. God, had she been hit? Sweet Jesus, no. Not this. Not now!

She dropped down beside her. The girl was crying. The girl was fine. She must have tripped, that's all. Thank God she hadn't been—

'On your feet! Both of you!'

Melanie did as she was told. They both did. She turned to face him and pulled the girl in close, throwing a protective arm around her small body.

'Are you going to let us go?'

He didn't answer.

'Are you?'

'Just let me think a while, dammit.' His voice was charcoal as he walked over. He reached into his pocket and produced the Ventolin inhaler. He couldn't speak; he allowed the gun to speak for him. She saw him pointing it at a patch of scrub. The girl sobbed. Who could blame her? He waved the gun again, breathing hard, and Melanie started to walk. The girl fell in beside her.

'You're trapped. The police will be everywhere by now.'

'Shut up!'

'Let us go and you might still make it.'

'Shut up, I said. We're family, remember?'

Melanie remembered. She risked another slap,

maybe something worse.

'You'll never make it if you don't let us go.'

'Keep walking, girls.'

They dragged themselves through the thin corridor of scrub, away from the ocean. He put away the Ventolin and forced them at gunpoint to start climbing a steep slope of sand. Halfway up, the girl fell, came tumbling back down. She blinked back the tears as he grabbed her by the arm and yanked her onto her feet.

'Walk! Do you want Monster to come back and eat you up!'

Melanie watched him bend down on one knee and brush away the sand from her face. For one horrible moment he reminded her of her father.

'Can't you see she's exhausted?'

'We're all exhausted! But we can't stay here.'

'Where are you taking us?' Melanie demanded. 'This is nowhere.'

'I'm trying to think, dammit.' He turned the girl around and sent her on her way. 'I have to get you away before Monster returns.'

Melanie waited for the girl. They held hands and resumed the long climb together.

'Stop. Wait.' He followed them up, great clumsy bounds, the soft sand sliding up past his ankles. 'I have a better idea. Kneel down.'

The girl obeyed. Melanie hesitated. There was her father again.

'Kneel!'

She could scoop a handful of sand, fling it in his face and run. Too late. He grabbed her shoulder, hard, and she found herself kneeling in front of the wall of sand.

'Close your eyes. Tight. Both of you.'

They did as they were told.

'Monster won't hurt you now. I won't let Monster hurt anyone ever again.'

'Who is Monster?'

'No talking.'

'Is Monster your mother?'

'I said—'

'It *is* your mother. God.'

'No, Mumma's dead. I made her die.'

'You mean you killed her?'

'I—'

'You murdered her? I don't believe you.'

'Hush now, Claudia. I know what happened. I know what the boys did, what Mumma was thinking.' His breathing sounded tight-chested. 'Don't worry. I stopped them. Stopped her!'

'Who is Claudia?'

At the sound of Melanie's voice he seemed to snap back. 'Just keep those eyes closed,' he said, angry now. 'I'll know if you open them.'

'Please let us go.'

'Mumma won't hurt you. No one will touch you ever again. You'll see.'

Melanie felt the shifting sand as he stepped back.

'Now I want you to say this prayer with me.'

Prayer? Get real!

'Now I lay me down to sleep.'

'Wait! You can't be serious.'

Beside her the girl mumbled his words, her voice barely a whisper.

'I pray the Lord my soul to keep.' Did he just take another step back?

'I pray—'

'That's right. Keep saying it, girls.'

'Please. Whoever you are, don't shoot. If you spare us, the police will go easier on you.'

'More videos, Melanie? Stick around, kid. I'll show you the real thing.'

Melanie waited for the awful moment but it never arrived. He moved quickly away back down the slope. At the sound of the panel van door slamming she seized her chance.

'Run! Quick!'

Together they clambered up the rest of the way, not daring to look behind. At the top of the tall dune they saw headlights way back in the distance. Melanie pushed the girl forward and raced down behind her. The slope fell steeply away to darkness but she no longer cared. Halfway down the girl lost her sneaker. Forget it. Forget him. Whatever had happened, he had no right to inflict his damage upon them. He could rot in hell for all Melanie cared, just as long as he didn't drag her and the girl along for the ride.

Crack!

At the sound of the single gunshot she dived to the ground, hauling the girl down beside her. Any moment now she would hear him.

She was wrong. The thunderclap lit up the night sky and rained burning debris all around. Melanie pushed the girl's head down, ignoring her cries until the moment passed.

'Stay here!'

She needed to know, charged back up the dune and down the other side. The panel van burned fiercely and by the time she reached it there was nothing she could do to save him. Intense heat pushed her back but it didn't stop her looking.

What did she see first, the flaming torch peeling

back his body or the fireball bandaged round his head? His face, no longer a face, was thrown up against the burning driver's seat. Was that the last remains of the monster mask she saw, now melting away his features forever? One hand was fused to the steering wheel, the other seemed to crush the gun. Both arms were on fire.

His head fell sideways in the seat and he seemed to grin at her one last time. She backed away, turned and fled. The burning vehicle cast leaping shadows as she ran.

WISH UPON A STAR

The steady *thwock-thwock-thwock* of the rotor blades finally lifted the police helicopter into the moonlit sky.

'Take us over the beach.' Beverley nudged the pilot's arm.

'Gotcha.' He took the helicopter up higher and thumbed the switch that turned night into day. Below them, in the car park of historic Ellendale Hamlet, Constable Ross Peters led the procession of three patrol cars out onto the North West Coastal Highway.

Further along the highway a large road train drove through the night; in the next hour it would pass through Geraldton to the north and carry on up the coast to Carnarvon five hours away. Geraldton's harbour lights took on a surreal appearance.

'Down there!' Leo pointed.

'I see them.' The pilot swung right.

In the large paddock below, fixed in the chopper's artificial sun, three kangaroos stood mesmerised. The spotlight drifted over them and there was no escape until the pilot swung left and started the first sweep across the dune system.

'Some country!' Beverley was reminded of Kosciusko and her early morning swim. Some day!

The spotlight drifted up the long slopes of sand, mushroomed into large blow-outs, pin-pointed the night. Down below, the three patrol cars snaked along the twisting narrow track. Once they reached the beach they would split up. Needle in a haystack stuff, but it was their best hope of finding Levine before daybreak.

'We're gonna look pretty silly if he isn't down there,' said Leo.

'Even sillier if he is and we don't bother to check.' Beverley knew the score; Levine could be anywhere by now. Or he could be keeping his head down.

The second sweep, following the coastal strip and the beach ten kilometres south, took them over a fishing party cooking up a feast by the water's edge.

'Crayfish! What's the bet?'

Caught in the glare, the small group below lifted their beers to the night sky. One excited child ran after the patch of daylight for a while, both arms waving, but soon the helicopter wheeled back over the dunes and into the dark places.

'I don't like it.' Leo sighed loudly. 'Why come here?'

'Why burn down a school?' snapped Beverley. 'Why put Patrick Warren in hospital? Just keep looking!'

He shrugged his shoulders again. She hoped Ross and the boys were having a better time of it.

Setting off for the distant highway was like setting out to sea. And wasn't wading into the crop a little like wading through water? No stingers but. How about goblins and fairies?

The tall thin stalks were surprisingly resistant; the hardy ears of wheat scratched her bare arms. Minutes passed. For the first time Melanie seriously wondered if she would ever make it to the other side. It had been a hot day and the soft dirt beneath her feet had trapped a lot of heat. How far? Kilometres. After the first half hour the girl couldn't keep still; she kept fidgeting about on her shoulders.

'I'm tired.' The small weight shifted. Again.

'When can we go to bed?'

Great. Now she was expected to conjure up a motel. Did the fairies of the field accept credit? Or should she turn back and grab the magic glitter wand she had seen on the floor beneath the glove box?

'Are we there yet?'

'Nearly. Can you still see the lights?'

She still saw the lights. She heard the ocean. Her one bare foot felt the wheat tickle her toes.

'They're called ears,' said Melanie. 'Do you think they hear us coming?'

'Silly.'

'Maybe this field is like a giant ear.'

Did it hear *him* coming? Did it listen to the bite of his shovel, a live, hissing thing as it cried into the good earth and embraced the darkness there. No escaping his madness. She remembered the horror of the church and the school. She tried to block out his leering, melting face back at the panel van, worse than any video.

'Stars,' said the girl. 'Lots of stars.'

Melanie glanced skyward. The night seemed to bounce to the rhythm of her walk.

'Moon.'

'I think we'll stop for a rest,' said Melanie, the

girl's weight storing up in her neck and shoulders.

'Juice?'

You wish.

The third sweep finally revealed something.

'Higher!' Beverley saw something, some distance away, back towards Geraldton. 'Over there!'

'I see it!' The pilot leaned the chopper in the right direction.

As he spoke the radio crackled into life. Beverley listened hard, clapped her hands when the message was received. Five minutes ago a school tour bus heading back to Perth had pulled up at the Dongara road block sixty kilometres south. Kids said they saw a red glow in the sky past the wheat fields near Ellendale Flats.

Soon they were hovering over the flames.

'It's them!' Beverley grabbed the handset and alerted the others.

The burning vehicle was parked alongside a small beach shack in an area of low scrub and tall dunes.

'We're right on the tail end of Southgates!' Leo stabbed the window. 'See! End of the track!'

Beyond the shack, stretching all the way north to the outskirts of Geraldton, the vast emptiness of the dune system hugged the coastline. Inland, however, the sand quickly gave way to a long, flat corridor of wheat that stopped at the highway.

'Can you take us down?'

'Low as I can go!' The pilot kept the chopper dragonfly still. 'Maybe back a ways I could manage it.'

Beverley patted his shoulder. 'See what you can do!'

'Been burning a while.' Leo studied the wreckage of the panel van. 'Lord, there's someone at the wheel.'

They rested a while. Melanie hadn't really noticed now many stars there were. Had she ever known the night sky to look so bold?

The stars come falling down on me tonight.

That was the message Peter Garrett pumped out on 'Outbreak of Love'. He wasn't fooling.

'Oh, look!' The shooting star was suddenly there, suddenly gone. The girl's small fist tugged the sleeve of her t-shirt. 'Make a wish! You have to make a wish!'

'I wish I didn't have to walk so far.'

'No, make a real wish!'

I wish Dad hadn't been so twisted. I wish Brad didn't have to order me about so much. I wish Mum would quit—

'Quickly, Melanie! You have to be quick!'

'Okay. I wish we were home. Your turn.'

'I wish we were home and I wish Heffalump didn't have to stay with the bad man.'

Melanie placed both arms around the girl and pulled her close. 'Hey, listen to me. It'll be fine. You'll see.'

'I don't like this place.'

'We'll be safe soon.'

'I'm tired.'

She hoisted the girl up onto her shoulders. 'Don't fidget.'

'Moon.' The girl stated the obvious.

'You like the moon?'

'It's round.'

'Yes.'

'Like on the phone to Mummy.'

Her words cut like a knife and Melanie couldn't speak.

Air. They needed to suck clean, cool air. All they got was the acrid stench of smouldering rubber.

'Back-up will be here soon, Ross. Don't worry.'

Beverley walked the constable away. 'There's a good chance they're still alive.'

They both glanced back at the panel van and the grotesque blackened shape slumped in the driver's seat. The arms and legs were almost burned away. The chest cavity no longer remained. But it was the head and the damage done there that caused Ross the greatest distress. The bullet, or the intense heat, or maybe a combination of both, had simply caused the head to explode.

'They say it gets easier, you know. With every body.' Again she pulled him away. 'But they only say that to try and make you sleep better at night.'

'I don't understand how he could just . . . how anyone could just sit there and not try to escape.'

'Oh, he escaped all right,' interrupted Leo. 'The moment he tossed that match behind his shoulder he escaped by pulling the trigger. I wonder what hit him first, the exploding jerry can or the bullet through the brain.' He stepped up for a closer look. 'Seen his face? Like he wore a mask or something.'

The young cop couldn't look anymore.

'Ross, I need you to stay in control. Will you do that for me?'

He flushed with embarrassment. 'I just need some air, that's all. I'll be fine.'

'Good. Because I need someone reliable in the search party.' Beverley looked back along the track to the chopper. 'You know the area better than most.'

Someone from Geraldton CIB called them over. When they reached him, over by some bushes, he shone his torch on the ground.

'Make any sense to you?' Leo switched on his own torch for a better look.

'Nothing makes sense anymore.' Beverley eyed the rising moon. 'Don't touch anything. Seal off the whole area.'

There, spilling out onto the sand from a yawning suitcase, their torch beams fell on the happy, sad faces of Melanie Spence and little Christine Webster. Several grotesque joke shop rubber masks and an X-rated video lay scattered nearby, along with bundles of unmailed letters. Every envelope was addressed to Claudia Levine.

'Sicko,' muttered the detective.

'Over here!'

They whirled round, watched the figure running, falling down the sand dune and through the scrub.

'Hurry!'

They all ran, following the officer back up the

steep slope of sand to stand next to him on the ridge. Five, maybe ten kilometres away beyond the sand dune and across large fields of wheat, Beverley saw northbound traffic heading for Geraldton.

'Don't you see it?'

Beverley looked to where the torch beam danced. A small child's sneaker lay partly submerged in the sand.

'I'm thirsty.'

I'm Melanie. Nice to meet you.

'I'm real thirsty. I want a juice.'

'I think I've got that message.' Melanie laughed. Not far now. She bouyed the girl's spirits by promising a brand new pink elephant.

'Heffalump,' scolded the small voice.

They could no longer hear the ocean. Now it was the traffic that encouraged Melanie to keep going, not to quit, never quit.

'Look!'

She saw. After an hour—or was it two?—they were almost there. The traffic was not much more than a floating string of lights, noiseless and without substance, but it offered hope.

She had no idea of the time. All she knew was

that the horrible man was dead and their nightmare would end once they reached the highway less than two hundred metres away. The vehicles averaged three a minute. The sight of them comforted her.

'Spaceship!' The girl pointed somewhere in the sky.

'Right.' That was all she needed, for some bug-eyed psycho aliens to land in the crop and take them to Planet Puke.

'Spaceship,' insisted the girl. 'Is Monster in the spaceship?'

A road train rushed past and seemed to snatch her words away. Real close now. Less than 150 metres.

'No. Remember our little talk? Monster can't hurt us anymore.' If only she knew! She changed the topic. 'How about a big bag of lollies if we don't mention Monster anymore? Sound fair?'

'Heffalump likes lollies. Mummy likes lollies.'

Melanie smiled. Maybe she had done too good a job at cheering her up. The kid was switching to overdrive.

'Tell you what. Soon as we get out of here we'll see about buying you two new Heffalumps.'

'But I only want *my* Heffalump.'

Tough assignment. 'Okay. How about the world's biggest juice?'

'Orange and mango!'

Right. The wheat seemed to be thinning out. It really was like crossing an ocean. Up ahead a car sped past, its tyres a fading hum on the bitumen. Fifty metres to go. She waved wildly at the next approaching car but they were still too far away and its headlights merely brushed past them.

'Is the spaceship still there?'

'Yep!' She giggled. 'Now it's even bigger!'

The headlights of an approaching car blinded them.

'Wave!'

They both waved and the car braked hard, pulling in off the highway to the dirt shoulder and stopping close-by. An elderly woman wound down the passenger-side window.

'My name is Melanie Spence!'

'Yes!'

'He wanted to hurt me! Hurt us!'

'Who wanted to hurt you?'

The driver, a man in his sixties, stepped out of the car and looked around.

'Wanted to kill us!'

'What on earth?'

The night sky exploded with noise and movement. Melanie and the girl both looked up, shielding their eyes from the blinding light. It pinned them there, kept them safe.

THE LORD'S DAY

Melanie's mother arrived on the morning flight from Perth. She looked physically and emotionally drained.

'Mrs Spence, my name is Beverley Cruz. We talked on the phone last night.'

'Is she all right?' Mrs Spence searched the terminal building.

'She's fine. Receiving the best of care.'

'Did he . . .'

'No. Believe me, your daughter is in great shape. She's resting up.' Beverley placed her arm round Mrs Spence's waist and steered her past a group of European windsurfers and out of the building. 'We can visit her now if you like.'

'When can she come home?'

'How does this afternoon sound?'

She seemed relieved. They reached the waiting Falcon and Beverley placed her overnight bag in the boot.

'Of course, major crime squad will have a lot of questions to ask. You understand.'

'No. I don't understand. I don't understand any of it.'

Beverley helped her into the car. 'Seat belt,' she said, before she could stop herself. 'Sorry. Force of habit.'

'But she is all right?'

'You can see for yourself.' Beverley started up the motor. 'We'll be there in no time.'

'What about the little girl?'

'Too early to tell. She's young, so maybe she'll cope. It's going to be a long journey back to normal, though.'

'And her mother?'

Beverley didn't like to think about the mother. What sort of damage had *she* sustained—beaten up in front of her daughter, taken out back to the garage, dumped in the stolen Camry sedan and left for dead?

'Mrs Spence, your daughter is in Room 19 on the first floor. She was still asleep when I left her. It's a good sign.'

'You mean you're leaving.'

'I'm needed back at the crime scene. Then I have to pack. By midnight we hope to be on the red-eye special to Melbourne.'

She arrived to find Melanie asleep in the nightgown Ms Cruz sent out for.

A nurse entered the room, carrying a large vase filled with roses. 'They're beautiful, Mrs Spence.' She placed them on the meals trolley at the foot of the bed and checked Melanie's chart.

'Is she okay?'

'Fine. She just needs plenty of rest.' The nurse moved over to the window. 'Here, I'll draw down the blinds.'

'Please. No.' She liked the view. The first thing Melanie would see when she opened her eyes would be the familiar world again: rooftops, trees, the sun shining.

'Okay. I'll drop by in a little while.' The nurse was already leaving. 'Oh, and I heard there's a fax for Melanie downstairs at the reception counter.'

Mrs Spence thanked her, sat in the chair next to the bed and squeezed Melanie's hand.

'Oh, Melanie. Was it so awful?'

Her daughter looked so peaceful lying there

with the natural light on her face. The cut above her eye wanted to heal quickly. She didn't think it would scar.

After several minutes she got up and left the room. Messages so soon? She caught the elevator back down to the ground floor. When the elevator doors slid open she saw a large sign pointing the way to the reception counter. She walked over.

'I was told there was a fax for my daughter. Melanie Spence.'

'Yes, of course.' The receptionist got up out of her seat and walked over to a large pinboard holding assorted messages and envelopes.

Behind her she heard the elevator doors open. A sudden babble of children's voices and running feet swept through the main lobby, the hospital entrance and out onto the lawns. She heard the elevator doors close again.

'Here you are.' The receptionist held out the fax.

'Thank you.' She took the message and started to walk away.

'Mrs Spence.'

She turned round and saw the receptionist looked embarrassed.

'I just wanted to say I'm glad they made it. Your daughter and that poor little girl.'

'Thank you. You're very kind.'

'It's just that when I heard the radio this morning—'

'It's okay. I understand.'

Outside, three young children played chasey. She turned her attention to the fax. Several of Melanie's friends had gotten together with Rachel and Angela and scrawled goodwill messages. She learned a lot. Gemma reckoned all boys crap on. Simmo claimed to be the magic mushroom king of the southwest. Wendy said she went to Geraldton last holidays and could Melanie say hi to Kenny at the Corner Surf Shop. It was that kind of fax.

The elevator door slid open and she quickly stepped back to allow two nurses, a doctor and several visitors to spill out into the lobby. She didn't look where she was going and bumped into someone behind her. She dropped the piece of paper.

'Oh—'

'No worries.' The tall, middle-aged man bent down to help her, almost fell. He was on crutches and his head was heavily bandaged.

'I've got it.' She picked up the fax and apologised. 'I'm such a klutz.'

'Melanie's mum, right?'

More visitors. She stepped aside to let them through.

'Couldn't help sneaking a peek.' He pointed to the fax.

He was no one she recognised and she felt uncomfortable. He must have sensed her unease.

'I'm Detective Senior Constable Patrick Warren. Sorry I'm late.'

In all the excitement she missed the elevator again. The doors closed and the visitors were gone.

'My fault.' He watched the small arrow above the elevator doors light up on first. 'We could always use the stairs. Good for the heart.'

She looked at his crutches. 'You're joking, right?'

'Yes, I am.'

Beverley ignored the speed bumps and the NO PARKING sign and pulled into the hospital set-down zone. Unbelievably, the first person she saw as she hurried through the main entrance was Patrick Warren. He had his back to her and followed Mrs Spence into the elevator.

'Patrick, wait!'

The elevator doors started to close.

'Patrick!'

He used a crutch to prop the doors open. His

expression quickly changed when she rushed across the lobby.

'Wrong boots! It wasn't him!'

'What?'

'It was a local fisherman! It just came over the police channel.'

'What are you saying?' Mrs Spence's thumb rested on the elevator button. Beverley ignored her.

'Patrick, stay here in the lobby until back-up arrives.'

'Oh, God!' cried Melanie's mother. 'It's him, isn't it?'

'Look, Mrs Spence, I need you to do something for me.' She stepped into the elevator. 'Find a nurse on Melanie's floor and tell them to shift her to the children's ward on the fourth floor. She'll be safe there. He might be crazy but he isn't stupid.'

'But I don't understand. You said—'

'I was wrong.'

'Oh, God.'

'Do as I say, Mrs Spence. I need you to come through for me.'

'Where will you be?' asked Patrick, already hauling himself back into the lobby.

'Room 27. Second floor. That's Christine's room.'

Patrick's thoughts were elsewhere. 'The

fisherman owned the golden labrador, right?'

'Yes.'

'And he drove some kind of off-road vehicle?'

'Later, Patrick.' She gently pulled Mrs Spence's hand away and the elevator doors started to close. 'Wait for back-up.'

'Please don't let him near my little girl.' Mrs Spence looked confused, scared. She rocked on her feet and her fists were small stones. When they reached the first floor she hesitated.

'Go find a nurse, Mrs Spence.' Beverley waited for her to get out. 'I'll go and get Christine and meet you in the children's ward.'

The elevator doors closed. Sweating now, her heartbeat a rising flood.

Melanie woke from uneasy dreams. She heard the sounds of things being put away and someone brushed past her bed. She squeezed one eye open, half expecting to see Betty Boop sitting on her dressing table. She saw the sky instead. That, and a nurse's uniform.

'What time is it?' Melanie opened both eyes and saw that she had the room to herself.

'Oh, you're awake. Good.' The nurse lifted up her wrist. 'Time? Nearly 10.30.'

'I feel hungry.'

'We'll feed you soon, I promise.'

'I'm thirsty.'

'Just lie still. I want to check your pulse.'

She did as she was told. The ceiling looked freshly painted and she turned her attention to the view outside. When the nurse finished Melanie asked, 'Where's the girl?'

'Next floor up. She's fine, I promise.'

Second promise. Melanie wondered if she should start keeping a diary. The day looked hot. Sunday. It could keep.

'Your mother was just here.'

'You mean they flew her up 'specially?'

'Of course they did. You're a celebrity.'

Melanie thought she heard children playing on the grass outside. She didn't think of herself as a celebrity. Her body ached all over and it reminded her of the long hours spent in darkness, the pain, her fear.

'Sit up then.'

Melanie welcomed the glass of water. She sat up and finished the drink while the nurse propped up the pillows behind her back. She noticed the portable tv for the first time, jutting out of the wall like some Spielberg eyeball.

'Better?'

But Melanie did not answer. In the tv's dull reflection she saw a familiar object. The empty glass slipped through her fingers and into her lap.

'Hey, careful.'

Above the end of the bed sat a large vase of flowers. Next to the vase sat a grubby pink elephant.

'They never forget, Melanie.'

At the sound of his voice the nurse spun round. He leapt at her from across the room.

DAMAGE

Monster wanted blood. It squeezed the nurse's neck.

'No! Let me think!'

Levine wiped down the pictures inside his head. He needed to think. Monster dismissed him. It saw only the thrill of squeezing, harder and harder, bone against bone, until something inside the windpipe cracked or popped or whizz-banged out, the framework teetering and buckling as it collapsed onto the shiny hospital floor.

'Stop it! You're hurting her!'

Monster heard Melanie—heard Claudia—and roared her down. Didn't she know it enjoyed hurting things, breaking things, being cruel? It altered the nurse's expression again. Fear to pain?

Pain to agony? No matter. It lifted her off the floor, a growing ball of energy spinning out of control. Don't stop. Never stop. It wanted to absorb the woman's damage, to taste her violent struggle. So many pictures now. Ready to explode.

'Creep!'

Melanie rushed forward, not thinking. She saw his eyes fix upon her and his hands let go of the nurse. The woman fell to her knees, coughing and choking, unable to breathe. He raised his boot and kicked her aside.

'Big bully!'

It was as if she couldn't stop herself. She marched up to him and punched him hard in the chest.

'Temper, temper, Melanie.'

'Leave us alone!' She punched him again and suddenly remembered lunchtime last Thursday when Brad showed up.

'Poor Melanie. Did you hurt your hand again?' Taunting her now.

'Go away!'

She went to hit him again. His hands flew down and grabbed her wrists. Hard. He pulled her arms down, just like when he'd forced her to watch that video. Even though she struggled and kicked, and even though the nurse struggled to breathe there on the floor beside them, he grinned down at her.

'What's funny, retard?'

'You're starting to disappoint me, Melanie.' He grabbed her around the waist and pulled her in close. 'Be good.'

Her mother appeared at the doorway.

'Stay back, Mum!'

'No, come on in, Mum. Join the party.' Suddenly he was dragging her across to the large window. 'Here, let me make more room.'

'Why are you doing this?' demanded her mother.

Melanie looked up, surprised. The question had been cold, calculating.

'Beats working for a living.' He pushed his knee into her back. 'Now if you'll just get out of my way—'

His words were shattered mid-sentence as Melanie sank her elbow into his groin. She swung back hard and low and did the same again. Before he could even recover she slammed the back of her head up under his chin. She felt his jaw crack sideways, repeated the act, once, twice, again and again. Her head hurt but she kept on going. She blinked back the pain, rubbed away a moment of dizziness only to see Ms Cruz back again, filling the doorway, shouting. She produced a gun.

Her mother shouted now. Melanie watched in slow-motion as she tried to pull the gun away. She saw the gun spit.

Crack!

The bullet broke the window; the window stole their balance. Melanie felt herself being hauled backwards as he fought to stay upright. She elbowed him again, as low and hard as she could, and he threw open his arms enough for her to twist round and push him off. He tried to grab hold of her and she jumped back to avoid the arc of his fists. Not fists. Two outstretched hands, clawing and scratching the air.

He fell backwards out of the window, roaring Claudia's name all the way down.

'Melanie, no! Don't look!'

She looked anyway. Broad leaves and thick foliage broke his fall and rolled him heavily onto the well-tended lawn. She saw him squeeze his eyes shut, as if to greet the fresh explosion of plain. The excited cries of children washed over him and for one sweet moment she thought he might choose to lie there and not move. He opened his eyes, stared right at her, and when she saw him work a cruel smile she knew she thought wrong. Two boys and a girl stood over him, curious as the wind. He hissed at them and they all ran away.

Something had happened. Moments earlier Patrick watched helplessly as some small kids raced each other through the undercroft, past Beverley's vehicle and round the side of the building. He shouted after them. When he tried to follow, he slipped and crashed heavily to the floor. He dropped both crutches and grimaced in pain.

The receptionist hurried over.

'Find out what's going on! It's important!'

She helped him sit up and hurried outside. While she was gone he managed to haul himself to his feet with one crutch and groaned loudly when he couldn't reach the other.

The receptionist returned a short time later, breathless and looking very pale. The three children fell in alongside her.

'They say a man fell through a first-floor window.'

'Is he okay?' Patrick looked for a clue from the children. They said nothing.

'I think I saw someone running off.' The woman

seemed to be going into shock. She walked over and handed him his other crutch.

Beverley Cruz rushed down the stairs on her way outside. 'Christine Webster's not in her room.'

Patrick turned back to the receptionist. 'Can you take the children somewhere safe? Upstairs?'

'To the children's ward,' added Beverley.

Now she looked confused, frightened, but she did as she was asked. She led all three children to the waiting elevator.

Patrick waited for the elevator doors to close. Beverley was outside on the lawn, already heading back toward him. Painfully, he dragged himself to the main entrance to join her. Samuel Levine would already be on his way. As for the little girl?

Beverley must have shared the same thought. 'It's over. He got away. He'll always get away.'

'I can't believe that. No one deserves that much luck.' He heard sirens.

Beverley stood facing him, real close. 'That'll be the troops.'

He shrugged his shoulders. 'Better move your car or they might give you a parking ticket.'

'Patrick—'

'Better lock it up, at least. Plenty of little kids

around.'

'That's not funny, Patrick.'

'Look.'

She looked. There, in the back seat, a small familiar face was pressed against the window. Beverley rushed forward, opened the car door, picked up the girl and hugged her tightly.

'Oh, good girl, Christine! We thought—'

'We thought you were going to miss out on seeing your mummy,' said Patrick quickly. 'She'll be wondering where you got to.'

Little Christine Webster's face seemed to brighten. 'Heffalump,' she whispered, pointing directly at him.

'Who? Me?'

He humoured her and pretended the crutch was a trunk. He almost fell over.

Moments earlier Melanie had grabbed the pink elephant, thrown a full-length towelling robe over her nightie and sprinted barefoot along the first floor corridor and straight down the flight of stairs. Her mother's shouts hadn't convinced her to stop. Nor had the fury of police sirens now tearing up Geraldton's sleepy Sunday morning.

What had she expected to see as she rounded the

corner? Anger. Frustration. Anything but the girl safely in the arms of Ms Cruz.

'Heffalump!'

The polished floor felt cool underfoot. Melanie nodded to Ms Cruz and tiptoed her way to the cop. She placed the pink elephant on his shoulder.

'Hey!'

'Suits you, Patrick.'

Ms Cruz let the girl down and she rushed over to claim her property. Flushed with embarrassment, her boss was happy to oblige.

'Mine.' She practically ripped it out of his hands and hugged it tight.

'Hi there, Christine.' He roughed her hair. 'Nice to meet you.'

Christine. So that was her name. In all the excitement of last night Melanie had forgotten to ask.

'See, Melanie!'

Melanie saw Heffalump squeezed in a headlock, its trunk crushed under her arm.

'Silly Heffalump.' She sounded subdued. 'He thought the bad man wanted to keep him.'

'Silly,' said Melanie, ice running through her veins. Across town the police sirens got louder, like baying dogs, and suddenly she wanted to ask a thousand questions. Who was he? Where did he come from? And who was Claudia?

'Will Mummy be angry?' asked Christine, to no one in particular.

'No, never.' Melanie spoke quickly. 'She'll be *really* happy.'

Satisfied, the girl took her by the hand and they followed Ms Cruz across the lobby to the elevator.

'Hey, what about me?'

'Relax, Patrick. You can take care of the cavalry while I try and find the girls some clothes.'

The elevator doors slid open. Melanie caught her mum's astonished look.

The pink elephant was held up for her to see.

'This is Heffalump and Mummy says I can take him to Disneyland.'

Melanie wished she had a camera. She laughed. She didn't mean to, but she laughed anyway. For one brief moment her laughter was enough.

'Silly.'

Three patrol cars pulled up, their sirens ugly with noise. They threatened to take away her laughter. Never. She needed the courage to laugh loud, wash clean, let go. Why be a victim when she could be a survivor?

'We got him!' The young constable could hardly

contain himself as he ran into the lobby. 'I mean, Leo got him! It just came over the radio. He was driving an old Land Rover.'

'Good for you, Ross.' Beverley steered Patrick into the elevator. 'I'm glad.'

'So much for being the tough cowboy,' continued the excited voice. 'He never said a word as they snapped the handcuffs on.'

'Levine was no cowboy.' Patrick spoke up, his serious old self. 'He was a little boy who got the stuffing kicked out of him.'

Christine Webster squeezed Melanie's hand tight as they stepped into the elevator and waited for the doors to close. 'He's gone?' she said, her voice a whisper once more. 'The bad man's gone?'

Melanie looked at her mother, and said nothing.

EPILOGUE

'I have tried to scream, but nothing will come out of me. No sound, no noise, no nothing.'

Brian Keenan,
who spent four-and-a-half years as a hostage in Beirut

BACKLASH

Three days, the longest three days of Melanie's life.

Last night on the news they'd shown the wheat fields out past Ellendale. They'd also shown the spot where that afternoon the police had recovered human remains. A police spokesperson had refused to speculate.

Claudia.

Watching the bulletin, Melanie had felt strangely detached, as if none of it was real. Even when the news camera panned to the abandoned church she'd felt nothing. No pain. No anger. What was she supposed to have felt?

But now she was back, functional, ready to walk into Plains Video and get even. It was childish but she didn't care.

She stepped off the painted pavement with its corny universe of Hollywood stars. Plains Video was almost empty. The girl behind the counter looked up and dismissed her as she squeezed through the turnstile and into the store. She wasn't the one. Brad's new girlfriend wore her hair long and blonde. Ever since Rachel told her what happened she had tried to bury her anger.

An archway led to the restricted section, where so many titles lured the imagination. Melanie paused to run her fingers along the shelves. How many movies? A hundred, two hundred?

Behind her, back at the counter, she heard someone talking and when she turned round there was the new girl, eighteen and sexy, her hair longer and blonder than she had imagined. No wonder Brad had made his move. Standing alongside, processing a tall stack of videos, her workmate looked ordinary.

Melanie turned back to the shelves. She felt used just looking at the covers. The presentation was anything but cheap. She wondered how many millionaires lived off the wall of titles that now confronted her. Hypocrite. She practically lived for movies. And only days ago she had almost surrendered and shown Brad something hotter, slicker, more explicit.

Quickly, before she changed her mind, she grabbed half a dozen videos from the bottom shelf and headed back to the counter. She clutched them to her chest, like some 1950's American bookworm clutching the classics after a trip to the library.

Brad's new girlfriend saw her coming and reached for the scanner. Clearly she did not recognise her, or if she did she played it very, very cool.

'I'm the schoolgirl.' Melanie paused by the counter just long enough to get the message across. 'You know, the celebrity.'

Now she registered. 'Oh, wow. You're the one who got—'

'Abducted. Right. And you're the girl who stole my boyfriend.'

'Hey, look, I'm real sorry about that.'

Melanie didn't stop. 'It's okay. Really. You deserve him. He's such a low-life scumbag.'

The other girl stopped what she was doing and called after her. 'Hey, have you got your membership card?'

'Not any more.' She hurried away. 'I'm a reformed addict.'

'Hey!'

She dashed through the security grille and out onto the pavement. The system activated, sending out a loud *beep*.

'Hey, stop!'

Melanie removed the top video cassette from its gaudy cover and proceeded to spool out the tape, fast, faster, an arm length at a time.

'Stop that!'

A man's voice. When she heard heavy footsteps behind her she ran, along the pavement and out into the car park where a middle-aged woman braked sharply to avoid her.

Melanie laughed, ran behind the car and to the side of the road. The traffic was heavy and she was glad. She tossed the videos across both lanes, watched as a passing truck cleaned up two titles and several cars destroyed the other four. The video cases cracked open like brittle shells, shooting plastic and magnetic tape into the kerb.

'What are you doing?' shouted a voice beside her.

Melanie looked up as if from a dream. The middle-aged woman was there, her car still running, the driver's door left open.

'I'm getting even.' And even as she said the

words Melanie saw a long tangle of ribbon caught on a disappearing bumper bar.

'Are you okay?' This time the woman sounded concerned, anxious. She touched Melanie's shoulder.

'No, I'm not okay,' said Melanie matter-of-factly. 'But that's not the issue.'

The girls from Plains Video arrived, accompanied by the store manager. Nosy shoppers gathered outside Ashmere Shopping Centre to gawp.

'What's going on?' he demanded, breathing hard and seeing the mess on the road. 'What's your problem, girlie?'

'No problem.' Melanie smiled at him, smiled at them all. 'Now I can go home.'

'Hey, wait a minute!'

Slowly, and with as much dignity as she could muster, Melanie stepped past them and walked away. She ignored their noise, their clutter, their passing judgment. What did they know?

Glyn Parry left school early to become a fighter pilot, but only made it as far as the local youth group. There he met a girl who laughed at his jokes so he ran away with her. Now he has a wife, three children, two dented surfboards and sand in his ears. When he isn't going over the falls he lives in outer space, where he writes teenage books and dreams of surfing the main break on a Nat Young original. For further adventures, check out your local bookshop.